MR. WALKER WANTS TO KNOW

Mr. Walker, the Cockney rag and bone man, is always bumping into other people's troubles. After the murder of old Cartwright in the jeweller's shop, he becomes involved in adventures with his friend Inspector Wedge of Scotland Yard, with the arrest of a crooked police officer, and the escape of Cartwright's killer. Then there is another death — in Mr. Walker's own sitting room — but his problems are just beginning, as he discovers that he himself is a candidate for murder!

ERNEST DUDLEY

◆

MR. WALKER WANTS TO KNOW

Complete and Unabridged

LINFORD
Leicester

First published in Great Britain

First Linford Edition
published 2007

British Library CIP Data

Dudley, Ernest
    Mr. Walker wants to know.—Large print ed.—
Linford mystery library
    1. Murder—Investigation—England—London—
Fiction 2. Junk trade—England—London—
Fiction 3. East End (London, England)—
Fiction 4. Detective and mystery stories
5. Large type books
I. Title
823.9'14 [F]

ISBN 978-1-84617-981-5

Published by
F. A. Thorpe (Publishing)
Anstey, Leicestershire

Set by Words & Graphics Ltd.
Anstey, Leicestershire
Printed and bound in Great Britain by
T. J. International Ltd., Padstow, Cornwall

This book is printed on acid-free paper

To darling Jane
with all my love
and

FOR GORDON CRIER

With grateful affection — in which
you, Dear Reader, should join,
because quite definitely if it hadn't
been for Mr. Crier, you wouldn't
have got your 'Mr. Walker'

1

'Any old rags, bottles, or bones . . .'

'Any rags, bottles, or bones . . .'
The voice calling out these words was a rich and fruity one, seeming to suggest to its hearers its owner was the sort of man who could be trusted. It was a voice inviting confidence, and it brimmed over with kindly understanding.

'Any old rags . . .'
In a moment the owner of this singular voice appeared round a corner and trundled a barrow into the busy Camberwell Road. He was a stout man of medium height with a round genial face, reddened by exposure to all sorts of weather. Around his twinkling eyes the laughter-lines were deeply carved. But though his eyes laughed so much there was a keen shrewdness behind them.

A battered bowler hat was pushed on the back of his head. A shabby coat

1

draped his ample form. His barrow was old and rickety and piled with a motley collection of old saucepans, books, clothes, shoes, two or three bicycle parts and a clock or two — the whole assortment surmounted by a stuffed bird in a glass cage. In other words it was a barrow-load of junk.

Against the background, noisy and bustling, of electric trams, buses and cars passing back and forth, the large man with his barrow stood out. There was no escaping him, for he was in short a man with a personality.

Keeping close to the kerb he trudged cheerfully along, missing nothing that was happening around him, his good-humoured face beaming as he exchanged cheery greetings with passing acquaintances. And there were many, for Mr. Walker was a well-known figure in that district, as well-known as he was in the more sophisticated surroundings of the West End of London and squares of Kensington and Mayfair.

Latterly, too, his voice had been heard in millions of homes up and down the land — this time through the medium of radio. Once a week, the junk man took radio listeners into his confidence and broadcast to them a human problem that he had encountered on his daily round.

Mr. Walker's lovable personality, his shrewd insight into the depths of the human heart, had won him millions of radio friends, or 'chums' as he called them. Of those 'chums' he knew personally were numbered all types of humanity, in every strata of society. From bricklayers to doctors, journalists to stage-door-keepers, barmaids to society hostesses, actresses to shop-girls. He had made the acquaintance of crooks and adventurers — big-time and small. He counted among his friends police-constables and sergeants, plain-clothes men and crime reporters. Whilst one of his best 'chums' was a detective-inspector at Scotland Yard.

Oh, yes, Mr. Walker and his old junk-barrow got about a bit.

About halfway along the road, he saw ahead of him a crowd of people gathered on the pavement. Among them was the

3

unmistakable helmet of a policeman, and he sucked in his breath sharply as he surveyed the scene.

' 'Allo!' he muttered to himself. 'Wot's up 'ere, I wonder?'

Reaching the fringe of the crowd he left his barrow by the kerb, and using his bulk to advantage, contrived to edge his way among the knot of interested people.

'Wot's 'appened, mate?' he inquired of a thin man amongst the bystanders. 'Accident?'

'Move on, there!' Before the thin man could answer him the constable's authoritative voice rang out. 'Now, come along, please. We can't have this pavement blocked!'

The crowd began to disperse, and presently Mr. Walker found himself next to the policeman.

'Wot's all the excitement, chum?' he asked hoarsely.

'Hallo!' said the constable, who knew him. 'You still wanting to know, Mr. Walker?'

This was a reference to his radio broadcasts, which were called 'Mr. Walker

Wants to Know.'

Mr. Walker chuckled throatily.

'Born curious, I was. An' lumme, ain't I allus a-bumpin' inter things wot tickles me curiosity, as yer might say? Wot's all the 'ow-d'yer-do about?'

'Bit of trouble — in there.' The constable jerked his head towards a small jeweller's shop a yard or so away.

'Wot, old Cartwright's? Wot is it, a smash-an'-grab? Or a burglary?'

'Did you know him?' asked the policeman, and Mr. Walker was quick to seize upon the tense he used.

'Wotcher mean — did I know 'im? Lumme, 'e ain't dead, is 'e?'

The constable looked hurriedly round to assure himself that none of his superiors was within hearing.

'I'm not supposed to tell you this,' he said, in a low voice, 'but old Cartwright's been murdered. He was found this morning, in the little room at the back of the shop, shot through the head!'

'Murdered!' Mr. Walker muttered. 'Poor old beggar! Queer old chap 'e was. 'Oo done it, chum?'

'Don't know.' The constable shook his head. 'The Inspector's in there now. Seems to be a bit of a mystery. Nothing was stolen.'

'That's sorter queer, ain't it? Nothink stolen an' all them jools an' things lyin' about waitin' ter be took-like. Wot time was the old feller done in?'

'The divisional-surgeon said he must have been shot before three. After one and not later than three, he said.'

'Wot was 'e doin' there at that time?' Mr. Walker frowned thoughtfully. ' 'E don't live there. It's only a lock-up shop.'

'Like as not he stayed late on some business or other,' answered the policeman. 'How well did you know him?'

'Pretty well, chum. 'E used ter save all 'is old junk fer me, an' when I called fer it we'd 'ave a chat about things — '

'Look here!' interrupted the other. 'You'd better come with me and see the inspector. Maybe he'd like to have a word with you.'

'Anything ter oblige, mate, that's me all over,' Mr. Walker replied agreeably. 'Wot about me old barrer?'

'It'll be all right where it is for a bit. Come along.'

The policeman led the way over to the shop and tapped on the closed door. After a slight delay it was opened by another constable.

'Where's the inspector?' asked Mr. Walker's companion. 'I've got a chap here who knew old Cartwright fairly well.'

There was a whispered colloquy.

'Wait here a tick,' said the policeman, and vanished inside the shop. Mr. Walker waited, eyed curiously by people still lingering in the hope of discovering what was going on.

Presently the constable reappeared.

'Come on in,' he said, and Mr. Walker stepped across the threshold into the gloom beyond.

The shop was a small one. A counter ran down one side to the left of the entrance, with a glass top, under which was displayed a collection of cufflinks, cigarette cases, and silver napkin rings. Behind the counter, and also covering the opposite wall, were glass-fronted cases that reached to the low ceiling. They were full of the usual kind of stock that a jeweller carries. At the far end, facing the door to the street, was another door, leading into a small room at the back of the premises. When Mr. Walker entered, this door was open, and in the room beyond stood two men talking together in low tones. One he recognised as the local inspector. Lang his name was. The other was a burly, thick-set sergeant.

'Come in, Walker!' called Divisional-Inspector Lang. 'I understand that you knew this man Cartwright.'

Mr. Walker admitted it.

'What did you know about him?' asked the inspector.

'Well, chum, 'e was a nice, friendly sort of old bloke. Always ready fer a chat. Reckoned as 'ow 'e was a bit lonely-like, I did. You know, glad for someone wot 'e could 'ave a bit of an 'eart-to-'eart talk with now an' ag'in.'

The inspector shot a quick glance at his sergeant.

'I suppose Smithson told you what has happened?' he said, and, before Mr. Walker could reply: 'Cartwright was

8

murdered early this morning. He was shot dead in this room by somebody who broke in through the back. It wasn't a professional job, but the murderer knew enough to wear gloves. Nothing was stolen, so far as we can make out from an examination of the stock-book, and the crime looks as if it has been committed by someone who had a grudge against the old man. Can you remember anything in these chats you used to have with him that might help us?'

Mr. Walker screwed up his rubicund face in an effort of memory. Finally he shook his head.

' 'Fraid I can't, mate. 'E didn't talk much about 'isself at all. Just wot yer might call odds and ends.'

'Did he ever mention the names of any of his friends?'

'Don't think 'e 'ad many, chum,' answered Mr. Walker. 'But now I come ter think about it, 'e did say somethink once about a nephew. Bloke 'e called Roy. Proper upset, 'e was, too, about something this chap 'ad done — '

The sergeant interrupted him, speaking to Lang.

'We must find this nephew,' he grunted and, turning to Mr. Walker: 'What was the trouble between them, d'you know?'

'Somethink about a girl, an' this feller Roy bein' an ungrateful 'ound.'

'A girl, eh?' The inspector pinched his nose between a thumb and forefinger. 'Did he mention her name?'

'No,' replied the junkman. ' 'E didn't say much about it at all. Only sort o' rambled on, as you might say. Jest grumblin' an' mutterin'.'

'H'm!' said Inspector Lang. 'You don't happen to know this nephew, do you?'

'No, chum, I don't,' answered Mr. Walker. Several more questions were put to him concerning the dead man, which he answered to the best of his ability. His name and address were taken, and he was led gently to the door and handed over to his friend the policeman. From first to last he had seen nothing of the body, except a sheeted shape on the floor of the little room.

As he emerged into the street a police

10

car drew up at the kerb and half a dozen men got out carrying small attaché cases and a large camera. The fingerprint experts and the official photographer had arrived.

Mr. Walker watched them go in, exchanged a word with the constable, and then, collecting his barrow, continued on his way. And with him, invisible at his elbow, stalked danger, for amid that pile of junk that heaped the barrow high, had he but known it, was the one clue that would have revealed the identity of the old jeweller's murderer!

2

Mr. Walker meets a problem

'Shop murder. Man detained!'

The newspaper placards outside the shops, and clutched in the hands of the news-vendors, bore the announcement in heavy, black type, and the throng of homeward-bound workers paused in their desperate rush for trains, buses and tubes to snatch eagerly at the copies of the evening papers that were thrust towards them.

'Got him, have they?' remarked a man to his friend. 'Well, that's pretty smart work! The murder was only discovered the day before yesterday! Just shows you — '

'There's our bus!' interrupted the other, and in the scramble that followed, the efficiency of the police and everything else was, for the moment, forgotten.

Helen Ford saw the flaring contents-bill as she left the little hat shop in which she worked, and bought a paper from a newsboy who was passing. In the light from a shop window she read the half-column below the banner headlines with a face that had gone as white as the newspaper itself.

'The police have detained Roy Morris for further questioning in connection with the murder of the elderly jeweller, Alfred Cartwright, who was found shot dead in his shop in Camberwell Road on Tuesday morning last. Morris is the dead man's nephew, and the police are said to be dissatisfied with his statement . . . '

The printed page danced and shook before her eyes. They had arrested Roy on suspicion of having killed his uncle, and unless she could prove that he hadn't . . . She shivered. And she knew he hadn't!

She stood in the light from the shop window, the paper clutched in her hand, trying to sort out her chaotic thoughts. The people who passed her stared curiously, but she was oblivious of their existence. The nightmare situation into which Fate had pitchforked her rendered everything else unreal. What was she to do? What could she do? The arrest of Roy Morris was a bombshell that had shaken her to the core and left her white and trembling. What could she do? What ought she to do?

The questions whirled round and round in her head until they acquired a diabolical rhythm that was like the beating of a drum. Mechanically she moved away towards her home, her brain controlling the actions of her limbs without conscious volition. If only there was someone to whom she could take her problem and seek advice. But its very nature made such a course impossible.

She came to the little house in which she lived and let herself in with her key. Her father would not be home until late, for which she was grateful. She wanted to be alone to think.

She went out into the neat little kitchen and made herself a cup of coffee, carrying it back into the sitting room. She had no desire for food. The thought of it made her feel sick. Sipping her coffee, her eyes wandered to the radio in the corner.

The news would be on soon. Perhaps there would be something about Roy. She got up and switched the set on. The burst of music startled her.

'Day after day,
I'm on me way,
Any rags, bottles, or bones?'

And then those rich, fruitily familiar tones:

'Good evenin', chums — '

Helen stared at the radio cabinet as though it had been a ghost. Mr. Walker! Mr. Walker, who every week dealt with just such a problem as was troubling her!

'Funny, ain't it, the queer things yours trooly bumps into — '

Mr. Walker! Could she take her problem to him?

She knew him, but dare she trust him? The deep voice, full of human kindness, droned on, forming a background to her thoughts. There was something so comforting about that voice, something reassuring.

'Jest drop me a postcard, will yer,

15

chums? And write on it: 'Tell 'er', or 'Don't tell 'er' — wotever you'd do, chums. See? Now, don't forget — Mr. Walker wants ter know — '

She had already made his acquaintance, for she had often encountered him and his barrow on her way to work in the morning. His quick, genial smile and hearty 'good morning' with which he'd grown used to greeting her, always made the start of the day cheery and bright for her.

Perhaps he could help her, Helen told herself. Anyway, she could put the thing to him as a hypothetical case — she needn't give anything away. She went to bed feeling a little lighter in spirit. There was someone who could help her.

★   ★   ★

'Wotcher, miss!' Mr. Walker's rubicund and genial face broke into a beaming smile of greeting as Helen hesitated, and then stepped beside him. 'Nice mornin' — ain't it?'

'Very nice,' she replied. 'Mr. Walker, I

wonder — could I speak to you — in private somewhere?'

'Why o' course yer can, miss. Anythink ter oblige, that's me all over. Wot about a cup o' corfee over there, eh?' He indicated a little teashop across the road.

'If you could spare the time, I'd be grateful,' she said eagerly.

'Spare the time? Why, bless yer, I'd take the whole blinkin' day orf to oblige a pretty girl like you.' Mr. Walker pocketed the pipe he had been smoking and turned his barrow round. 'You just pop acrost, see, an' I'll foller with me old chariot.'

She obeyed and waited for him on the opposite pavement, where, after carefully covering the contents of his barrow with sacking, he joined her.

'Come along, chum,' he said, leading the way into the café. 'We'll 'ave the 'ole blinkin' place to ourselves at this time o' the mornin'.'

He was right, for the place was empty. Finding a seat for the girl, he hailed the aged proprietor in a voice like a husky foghorn.

'Wotcher, chum! Let's 'ave two corfees

— an' see they're 'ot! . . . Deaf as a blinkin' post 'e is,' he confided to Helen in a lower tone as he sat down opposite to her. 'So yer can say wot yer like in front of 'im. Now, wot's the trouble?'

'It's not really any trouble,' she said untruthfully, and her cheeks reddened slightly as she told the lie. 'The fact of the matter is, I'm — I'm — er — well — I'm writing a book, and I want you to tell me what you think the heroine ought to do in the position I've put her in.'

'Writin' a book, are yer?' said Mr. Walker. 'Well, now, you tell me all about it an' I'll try an' 'elp yer.'

Helen waited until the old man who shuffled over with their coffee had gone again, and then she went on:

'Well, this is the situation, Mr. Walker. An old man is murdered, and this girl — the heroine in my story — knows who killed him. She's engaged to be married to the dead man's nephew. The police arrest him for the murder of his uncle, but she knows he didn't do it. She can only prove this by implicating her father, who is guilty. What ought she to do?'

18

'Lumme!' Mr. Walker said. 'You 'ave got a bit of a teaser, ain't yer? If she saves 'er sweetheart, she 'angs her father. An' if she keeps 'er mouth shut, the boy friend'll probably 'ang! I've 'eard a few narsty problems in me time, but this one fair takes the blinkin' biscuit.' He pondered for a moment or two.

'Dunno wot ter suggest. Fairly got me guessin', you 'ave. O' course, wot she ought ter do is go to the perlice an' tell the truth — '

'And hang her own father?' said Helen in a low voice.

'Well, I don't see 'ow she can let an innercent feller suffer for a crime wot 'e ain't never committed,' said Mr. Walker, shaking his head. 'That'd be even worse now, wouldn't it? Yer, see, arter all, although 'e's 'er father 'e is guilty. But the other feller, 'e ain't done nothink.'

'I suppose you're right,' said the girl, playing with her spoon. Mr. Walker took a prodigious gulp of scalding coffee.

'I can't think of no other answer,' he declared. 'I suppose, bein' as 'ow this is a story an' not real-like, yer couldn't make

19

it that she on'y thinks it was 'er father wot killed this 'ere feller. That'd be a way out, wouldn't it?'

'But I saw — ' she stopped herself quickly. 'Yes, that would be a way out,' she finished lamely. Her eyes met Mr. Walker's and dropped before his shrewd gaze.

'Tell yer wot,' he said, swallowing the remains of his coffee, 'I'll turn this problem o' yours over in me 'ead while I'm on me rounds, see? Maybe I'll 'it on somethink.'

He rose to his feet, bellowed to the deaf proprietor, and when he came, paid the bill.

'There ain't no need fer you ter 'urry,' he said as the girl started to get up. 'You stop 'ere an' drink yer corfee. You ain't started on it yet.'

She had forgotten all about it until he reminded her.

'I'll be gettin' along.' He pulled his ancient coat round his ample form and tightened the coloured neckerchief at his throat. 'So long, miss,' he said, and was gone.

Helen sat on, sipping her coffee. Mr. Walker's solution was, of course, the only one. She couldn't save her father at Roy's expense, and yet it was a terrible position to have to choose. What would Mr. Walker say, she wondered, if he knew that the situation that she had outlined was not fictional but real? She rose at last and left the little café.

And the man who had slipped in as the junkman made his exit, and taken an unobtrusive seat at one of the marble tables, followed her out.

3

Introducing Inspector Wedge

Inspector Wedge sat in his office at Scotland Yard and chewed at his long, ivory cigarette-holder, He was tall and thin. From the high dome of his forehead scanty and greying hair receded, and jet-black, bushy eyebrows jutted out from his long cadaverous face, giving him an almost Mephistophelian appearance.

His unblinking gaze was fixed upon Mr. Walker, whose great bulk overflowed the chair he occupied opposite him. The junkman's round rosy face made a sharp contrast to the other's saturnine features, and his rumbling gin-and-fog vocal tones mixed oddly with Inspector Wedge's quiet, nasally incisive voice.

Mr. Walker was beaming like the morning sun at his companion, as he sat there, clutching in one huge ham of a hand his dilapidated and shapeless bowler hat.

'Lumme, chum!' he was saying, ' 'tain't 'arf a long time since I larst saw yer, it ain't. D'yer remember that evenin' wot we spent down at that ware'ouse in Wapping? Didn't 'arf 'ave some fun, didn't we, mate?'

Inspector Wedge nodded, a faint smile illuminating his sardonic face. He recalled the evening very well. Though it hadn't been so amusing from his point of view. But for the robust intervention of Mr. Walker at a critical moment, his interest in that particular case upon which he was engaged — and in fact his interest in his entire future — might have ended there and then.

His companion chuckled reminiscently. 'Well, anyway, 'ow you bin getting' on?'

'Not so badly,' answered the detective. 'How's the world been using you?'

'Mustn't grumble, mate,' said Mr. Walker cheerfully. 'I've 'ad me ups an' downs since I see yer larst, but, takin' it all round, pretty rosy. An' the things I've bumped up against! Matter of fact, it was somethink wot I 'eard this mornin' 'as brought me round 'ere to see yer.'

The other looked interested. The problems that Mr. Walker 'bumped into' were always worth hearing.

'Tell me all about it,' he said encouragingly.

'Well,' began Mr. Walker. 'you know this shop murder?'

'You mean Cartwright, the old jeweller?'

'S'right. Well, it's about this feller, Morris, wot's bin arrested, wot I've come ter see yer.'

He had thought it all out very deliberately before deciding late that afternoon to call upon his old friend at Scotland Yard. And he felt sure that in doing so was the best way to help him to help Helen Ford and solve the problem that confronted her.

Not for a moment had her story about her writing a book deceived him. It had not taken him long to find the connection between her pitiful string of lies and the shop murder — for he knew of her engagement to Morris.

24

But most of all he could count on his detective friend for his sympathetic as well as his shrewd diagnosis of the case. He knew that beneath the other's sardonic exterior was a deep understanding of human foibles and frailties, a warm and ready sympathy for anyone deserving of it. So that Mr. Walker had no hesitation in putting all the cards on the table before Inspector Wedge.

'Yer see, chum,' he went on, 'this chap Morris was old Cartwright's nephew. Got a girl called Helen Ford, 'e 'as. Nice little thing she is — knows me — and this mornin' she pitches me a queer yarn.'

He proceeded to relate his interview with the girl at the café.

'O' course, 'er story-writin' didn't cut no ice with me, chum,' he concluded. 'There wasn't no doubt in my mind that wot she was a-tellin' me was real, see? Now, wot's bin botherin' me is — wot oughter be done about it? Yer see, I advised 'er ter go ter the perlice an' tell 'em wot she knows. But will she? An', if she don't, wot ought I ter do? Tellin' me this 'as made me a sort of an accessory, if

25

yer knows wot I mean?'

With deliberate care Wedge fitted a fresh cigarette into his holder.

'If this girl really knows it was her father who killed Cartwright, and not Morris,' he said gravely, 'there's no question she ought to inform the police immediately. Apart from making herself an accessory after the fact by keeping silent, she is endangering the life of another.'

Mr. Walker nodded. 'That's 'ow it struck me. O' course, yer can understand 'er feelin's. Blood's thicker than wot water is every time, an' natcherly she don't want ter go an' give 'er own father away, but this young feller's got ter be thought of as well, ain't he?'

'Most certainly!' agreed the detective.

'Well, that's wot I came to you for, chum,' said Mr. Walker. 'Seein' 'as 'ow this girl 'ad taken me into 'er confidence, like, I didn't wanter go ter the first perliceman I sees, so ter speak. But with you I know I'll be all right. I come ter you as the right bloke ter do it.'

'I'm very glad you did, Walker. It's a

very interesting problem. You see, if this girl is so sure her father killed Cartwright, the question arrives as to why is she so sure? Did he tell her, or did she actually see the crime committed?'

A cell of memory in Mr. Walker's brain opened suddenly.

'While she was a-talkin' ter me,' he said, 'she sorter made a slip-like. Yer see, I didn't let on as 'ow I didn't believe this story of 'ers that she was tryin' ter put acrost about writin' a book. An' I says: 'Couldn't yer make out she only thinks it was 'er father wot killed this feller — talkin' about this girl in the story, you see, chum? An' she answers, quick-like: 'But I saw — an' pulls 'erself up sharp.'

'Which seems to suggest she saw the murder,' murmured Wedge. 'And that brings up another question. If she saw the murder, what was she doing at Cartwright's shop at that hour of the night? I think we might see this girl and try to persuade her to tell us the truth about the whole business. We'll be doing her a kindness in the long run.'

'Anythink you says, chum,' agreed Mr. Walker readily.

'Do you know where she is to be found?'

'Well, she lives in Pelham Street, jest orf the Commercial Road, an' she works at an 'at shop, not a stone's throw from Cartwright's.'

'That's where she would probably be now,' said the detective, glancing at his watch. 'Suppose we slip along there now?'

Mr. Walker nodded, and the other rose. As he moved over to get his hat and coat, he paused and took a cigar box out of a drawer in his desk.

'Try one of these to smoke on the way?' he suggested, and Mr. Walker took one of the cigars he offered with a wide grin.

He followed the detective out of the office and a few minutes later they were speeding in the direction of the Commercial Road, Mr. Walker puffing happily at the big cigar wedged in the corner of his mouth.

The hat shop where Helen Ford worked was a chromium-faced establishment with the name 'Lucille' in red neon tubes over it. Three hats of extraordinary and eccentric shapes, supported on slender, twisted columns, against a background of oyster-coloured silk curtains, graced the brilliantly lighted window. Their object seemed to be to testify to the extreme exclusiveness of the business carried on.

Inspector Wedge got out of the taxi, instructed the driver to wait and, with Mr. Walker at his heels, pushed open the plate-glass shop door. A gust of warm and highly perfumed air greeted him as he stepped inside and a buzzer burred softly. From behind a ground glass partition that formed a sort of cubbyhole at the back of the shop, appeared a woman.

She was tall and thin, with ash-blonde hair that was so perfectly set it might have been made from the metal which composed the greater part of the place. She came forward with an undulating movement that suggested her very high heels contained springs, and smiled a welcome. It was a smile that twisted her thin lips, but left her cold eyes hard and calculating.

'Good evening,' murmured the Scotland Yard man. 'You have, I believe, a Miss Ford working here — '

The smile vanished from the woman's face.

'What's happened to her?' she demanded in a rasping voice that was a little out of keeping with so much elegance. 'She should have come in this morning, and she hasn't been here all day. Is she ill?'

'That I can't tell you. I am not acquainted with her personally. I merely wanted to speak to her on a matter of business.'

'Well, she's not here,' said the woman. 'You'd better try her home. If you do see her you can tell me that if she isn't here at ten o'clock tomorrow morning, she needn't come again.'

She turned away abruptly and went back to her tiny office.

'Wot a lady!' observed Mr. Walker, when they were back on the pavement. 'Yer do meet 'em sometimes, don't yer, chum?'

Wedge nodded absently. 'How far is this girl's house from here?' he asked.

30

'About 'arf an hour walkin'. 'Arf a tick in that there taxi.'

'Come along, then.' The detective led the way back to the waiting taxi. 'Let's see if we have any better luck at the house.'

But the little, gloomy house in Pelham Street was in darkness, and repeated knocking brought no response.

'Nobody at 'ome,' said Mr. Walker.

'Apparently not. The question is, where is she?'

Inspector Wedge glanced at his watch, which registered in the region of six o'clock. He stood on the step, undecided. It seemed as though they'd had a wasted journey.

'Does she live here alone?' he asked suddenly.

'No, 'er pa lives with 'er.'

'Know him?'

'Can't say as 'ow I does. From wot I've 'eard 'e's a pretty bad lot, though. Bin 'inside' twice. That poor kid ain't 'ad none too easy a time, one way an' another, since 'er mother died. That was three year ago.'

'H'm . . . Well, it doesn't look as if it's

31

going to be any good staying here. There's no knowing when she may come home. It's strange she shouldn't have gone to work today, though. What time was it this morning that you saw her?'

'Nine o'clock — just on,' answered Mr. Walker. The act of speaking made him lose hold of the half-cigar, which was still stuck in the corner of his mouth. It fell, hitting the step with a shower of sparks. He moved a pace forward to pick it up, his foot slipped on the shallow doorstep, and, stumbling, he flung out a hand to save himself. The next moment he was sprawling in the passage of the house, for the door had given inwards under his weight, and swung back.

Mr. Walker gasped out a few choice epithets as the detective hauled him to his feet.

'Lumme!' he grunted breathlessly. 'The blinkin' door was open all the time, chum — '

He stopped and sniffed. ' 'Ere, can yer smell somethink — '

'Yes,' said Inspector Wedge grimly. 'Gas!'

4

Death in the dark

The narrow, dark passageway reeked with gas. Now the door was open it came billowing out in invisible clouds that caught breathtakingly at their throats.

'Crikey!' gasped Mr. Walker, retreating hastily. 'There mustn't 'arf be a big escape somewhere, chum — '

'I think there is.' And Wedge whipped a silk handkerchief from his breast pocket and tied it swiftly round his nose and mouth. 'I'm going in to see. You stay outside.'

He drew a torch from his pocket and flashed it into the passage. The light flickered on a hallstand, a chair, and, beyond, the bottom of a narrow staircase. Drawing a deep breath, the detective stepped across the threshold. Moving along the passage he found the gas grew thicker as he neared a door facing him at the side of the staircase. Opening this, he almost choked, for the fumes were stronger here than anywhere. But he managed to continue to hold his breath, though the effort made the blood drum and throb in his temples, and entered the room. It was a kitchen and from somewhere near at hand came a steady, gentle hissing.

He located the sound after a few seconds. It came from a gas cooker in one corner. Staggering over, the inspector saw the oven door was wide open and a dark shape lay sprawled on the floor with head and shoulders inside. His lungs were bursting, and his head felt heavy and dizzy as he fumbled for the tap controlling the gas supply to the oven, and turned off the poisonous stream. The hissing stopped abruptly and, stumbling to the window, he threw up the sash, and gulped in huge draughts of air.

He felt better almost at once and dashed back to that still figure by the stove. It was a man of middle age, and Wedge bent over him, intending to drag him to the window. But at first touch the detective knew he was too late.

The only thing to be done was to clear the air of those poison-laden fumes. Leaving the window open, Inspector Wedge made his way to the back door. It was locked, but the key was in the lock, and twisting it, he pulled the door wide, and as quickly as he could rejoined the anxious Mr. Walker.

'Wot 'ad 'appened?' that stout individual greeted him interestedly.

'Something pretty serious,' gasped Wedge.

He tore the handkerchief from his face and explained what he had found in the kitchen.

'Sooicide, eh, mate?' Mr. Walker whispered hoarsely.

'Looks uncommonly like it,' agreed the detective gravely. 'Whoever it is lying by that stove is dead all right. The gas must have been escaping for hours.'

'Must be old Ford,' said Mr. Walker, shaking his head. 'Lumme, it looks as 'ow 'e's solved this problem for us, don't it?'

'If it is Ford,' murmured Wedge. 'As

soon as the atmosphere has cleared, we can find out.'

At the expiration of half an hour the air in the house was breathable, although still heavy with the reek of gas. The detective, accompanied by Mr. Walker, once more entered the little kitchen. Finding the electric light switch, he put on the light, and went over to the stove. The man who lay face downwards with his head in the oven was shabbily dressed and wore a pair of dilapidated leather slippers. His hair was iron grey and cut very short to his head.

'That's ol' Ford,' orlright,' said Mr. Walker, staring down at the body. 'Luv us, it's goin' ter be a nasty shock fer that girl when she comes 'ome.'

Wedge nodded. 'Yes. Though in one way it may be better for her. It certainly clears the situation.'

He dropped on to one knee beside the still figure and felt one of the hands.

'Quite cold,' he murmured. 'He must have been dead some time. We'd better get hold of a doctor and the police as soon as possible. How far is it to the nearest police station?'

'Matter o' about ten minutes' walk, chum. Like me ter 'op orf an' tell 'em wot's 'appened?'

'I wish you would. Then I can stay here in case the girl comes back.'

'Rightcher are, chum,' said Mr. Walker.

He disappeared into the gloom of the passage and the detective was left alone with the dead man. He sat down on a kitchen chair beside the table and took stock of his surroundings. The place was very neat and clean, although there was evidence that money was not plentiful in the Ford establishment. Where was the girl, and where had she been all day? Why had Ford committed suicide? Had the girl told him that she knew he had murdered the old jeweller, and that she was going to tell the police what she knew? That would explain both his death and the girl's absence.

After seeing Mr. Walker that morning, she had decided to take his advice. Most likely there would be news of her at the police station. Perhaps she had already made a statement and been reluctant to come home and face her father. Or she may have been detained by the police. If she had seen the murder, she must have been present when it was committed, and that would want some explaining away. Yes, there was no doubt where she was. Her father had known, or guessed, what she was going to do, and had adopted this way out. It all fitted in very neatly. It would be interesting to know just why Ford had killed the old jeweller, and how the girl had come to be a witness of the crime. She, of course, would be able to clear that up. A very simple, rather sordid case. Nothing spectacular about it.

Inspector Wedge wished Mr. Walker and the police would hurry up. It was cold in the draughty kitchen, and the gas-scented air was none too pleasant to breathe. It had already given him a slight headache. Perhaps it would be as well to get a bit of fresh air. Moreover, he could smoke outside. There was no reason why he should remain actually in the house.

He got up and went to the front door, standing on the little step and staring out into the dingy street. He put a cigarette into his long holder, and then decided it might still be unsafe to strike a match. Gloomily clamping his teeth on the holder he resigned himself to waiting. He was still standing there when the police arrived, and the first person to get out of the car was Inspector Lang. While Mr. Walker joined the two detectives, Wedge gave a brief explanation to the newcomer.

'H'm, well, I thought we'd got the man who killed Cartwright,' said Lang, when the other had finished, 'but what you've told me puts a different complexion on matters. That is, of course, if what this girl says is true.'

'There appears to be no reason why she should have lied,' said Wedge. 'In fact, there is every reason why she should not. The position, as she described it, was not a very pleasant one. Hasn't she been to the station to make a statement?'

'No, we've seen no sign of her,' said Inspector Lang, shaking his head, and Wedge's dome of a forehead wrinkled. Where had the girl got to?

'Well,' grunted Lang, 'we'd better go in

and have a look at this feller. You there, doctor?'

'Yes, I'm here, and waiting.' A small man with glasses, carrying a black bag, came forward out of the shadows by the gate.

'Come on, then.' They entered the house, the little doctor following. Wedge, with Mr. Walker, Inspector Lang, and a constable brought up the rear.

The doctor's examination was brief.

'There's no doubt he died from the effects of gas poisoning,' he announced, when the body had been shifted clear of the stove. 'And he's been dead some time. A good four to five hours, in my opinion.'

Wedge made a rapid calculation. 'Which means he must have died somewhere around three o'clock this afternoon?'

The doctor nodded. Mr. Walker gave a nod, too, in appreciation of the detective's mental arithmetic.

'Or even earlier,' the doctor added.

'Well, I don't know that it matters much what time he died,' murmured Wedge. 'The fact that he's dead is the important thing. You'd better telephone for the ambulance,' he instructed the constable.

The policeman touched his helmet and hurried away. Mr. Walker remained in the background, watching and listening with a kind of benign interest as the machinery of the law, set in motion by his and his friend's arrival on the scene of the crime, quickly gathered momentum.

'We'll have to get hold of the daughter as soon as we can,' said Lang. 'Where do you think she can have got to?'

'I've no idea at all,' said Wedge.

'Maybe she's bolted,' the other offered. 'Came home — found her father dead, and got scared. If she did see him kill Cartwright she may have a very good reason for being scared, too. Makes her an accessory.' He nodded, and went on: 'Probably that's why the door was open. She forgot to shut it properly in her hurry.'

'Perhaps,' Inspector Wedge murmured absently. 'Got your 'murder bag' with you?'

'Yes, it's in the car. Why?'

41

'Just like to make sure of something. Could you fetch it?'

'Yes,' said Lang, and departed. When he came back with the bag, which Mr. Walker eyed speculatively, Wedge asked for the fingerprint outfit, took it, and knelt down by the body.

Lang looked on wonderingly. He said: 'There's no doubt about its being Ford, is there?'

'None at all, I should think,' replied the other, without looking up.

'Then what's the idea?'

'You'll see in a minute.' And very carefully the man from Scotland Yard took prints of the dead man's fingers. Next, he began to take impressions of his own fingertips, in this instance, however, contenting himself with those of his right hand.

When this was completed, he selected a bottle of white powder from the finger-print outfit, went over to the stove and dusted the oven-tap with the powder.

'A matter of precaution,' he explained. 'You see, I turned this tap off when I first came in. So there should be a print of my

42

thumb and index finger superimposed on Ford's prints.'

'Well, I expect there is,' grunted Lang. 'If you turned the thing off, there must be.' Under his breath he added: 'What's the use of wasting time proving the obvious?'

Wedge gently blew the surplus powder away and peered at the tap. Mr. Walker's eyes had never left him as he proceeded with his careful investigation, and now they were popping with anticipation and excitement.

'Sometimes,' Inspector Wedge said, and there was a change in his voice, 'one succeeds in proving something that wasn't obvious.' Lang reddened as he realised the other's sharp ears had caught his muttered remark. 'I've done so in this case,' proceeded Wedge smoothly. 'The print of my finger and thumb is here, but there's no other. We've all been mistaken. Ford did not commit suicide. He was murdered!'

5

The case is altered

The varying expressions on the faces of the three men who heard his quiet statement were almost comical. Inspector Lang's jaw dropped, and his eyebrows shot upwards. Mr. Walker's mouth formed itself into an O of amazement. The little doctor gaped and his glasses slid down the bridge of his nose, leaving him blinking blindly. A complete and sudden hush filled the air for as long as it might take to count three slowly.

The doctor was the first to find his voice. 'What do you mean?'

'What I say,' said the Scotland Yard detective. 'Ford did not commit suicide.'

'Lumme chum!' breathed Mr. Walker. 'Ow d'yer make that out?'

'Because, before I touched it, there were no prints on this tap at all. It had, therefore, been wiped clean after the gas had been turned on. There is no earthly reason why Ford should have done that, but every reason why someone who wanted to make this look like suicide should.'

Inspector Wedge searched for his long cigarette-holder which he had pocketed, and stuck it — minus a cigarette — into his mouth. 'If Ford had turned that tap on he'd have left his prints. It's murder, sure enough.'

Lang, who seemed to have been struck dumb, now spoke.

'But who the devil killed the man — and why?'

'I don't think the 'why' is difficult to find,' said Wedge. 'The murderer wanted us to think that Ford had committed suicide because it rounded everything off so neatly. Ford kills Cartwright, and then he kills himself. Could anything be neater? The whole case cut and dried and finished. And the real murderer goes free.'

'Are you suggesting now that Ford didn't kill Cartwright?' demanded Lang.

Mr. Walker eyed Wedge with renewed interest.

'Yes. Don't you agree with me? This

45

has turned all your preconceived ideas upside down, you must admit. And mine, too, for that matter. I thought this was just a simple case, but it looks like proving extremely complicated. Look where we've got to at the moment. A respectable old jeweller is found dead in his shop — shot through the head. His nephew, for reasons which I don't know, but which I should like to hear presently, is detained by the police under suspicion of having committed the crime.

'The girl he is engaged to becomes worried because she believes her father is guilty. She is so certain of this that she puts up a very weak story to our friend Mr. Walker here, so that she can ask his advice as to what she ought to do.'

'S'right!' came from the junkman.

'Seeing through the story and becoming rather worried himself, he comes to me,' went on Wedge. 'I suggested we should interview the girl together and try to persuade her to tell all she knows. We can't find her, but we find her father with his head in the gas oven — dead. He hasn't killed himself, but he's been murdered. So we end at the beginning.'

'Bit of a teaser, ain't it?' Mr. Walker said.

Lang gave the rotund junkman a withering glance.

'It means we've got to start all over again, I suppose,' he growled.

Inspector Wedge's mouth twitched.

'I'm very sorry,' he murmured apologetically, 'but you can't get away from the facts, can you?'

'No but there's more ways than one of interpreting them!' said the other. 'This fellow Morris may be guilty, after all. He's engaged to the girl, isn't he?'

Wedge nodded. Mr. Walker added his assent.

'Well,' continued Lang rapidly, 'supposing they're both in this together? Morris gets arrested for killing the old man, and the girl, in order to try to clear him, trumps up this story about knowing her father to be guilty — '

'And kills him, so's to make her story look true, or, at any rate, so's to ensure that it can't be disproved,' interrupted Wedge. 'Is that what you're getting at?'

'Fits all the facts, doesn't it?' replied Lang. 'And the girl's gone off somewhere, which looks as if she knew what had happened.'

'It fits the facts, so far as I know them. But it makes this girl out to be pretty bad — '

'Well, why shouldn't she be? Most of the women crooks have been worse than the men. You know that as well as I do. And she's in love with Morris, don't forget.'

Detective-Inspector Wedge rubbed his cheek gently with the tips of his fingers. There was no doubt Lang's theory was possible. It might, if Helen Ford was the right type, be the solution. He had never seen the girl, so it was impossible for him to judge.

'What d'you think, Walker?' he asked, turning to the junkman, who had been listening with a worried frown.

'Don't seem right, some'ow, ter me,' answered Mr. Walker, shaking his head. 'That girl was fair worried when she spoke ter me, chum, I give yer my early bird.'

'Of course she was!' broke in Lang. 'Her boy friend was in a thundering mess, and she'd hatched up a scheme to get him out of it. Worried! I'll bet she was worried!'

'Well, chum . . . I don't believe she done it. She ain't that sort, if yer knows what I mean. Nice little girl wot wouldn't 'urt a fly, an' as fer killin' 'er own dad — ' Mr. Walker pursed up his lips and shook his head again.

'*I* think it's as plain as a pikestaff!' insisted Lang. 'And the fact she hasn't been to work today or come home this evening makes it all the plainer.'

Mr. Walker opened his mouth to voice his further protest but Wedge spoke first.

'There I think you're wrong. The fact of her not coming home is the biggest point in her favour. Because if she had planned this as cleverly as you suggest she did, she would have come home and made the discovery. You must remember she had no idea we were coming here this evening. The natural thing for her to do, if she had killed her father and tried to make it look like suicide, would be to come home, find him, and give the alarm. So far as she knows, the longer she stays away, the longer it will be before the discovery is made.'

'S'right,' interjected Mr. Walker, with characteristic succinctness.

'She probably intends to do that,' said Lang. 'What's the time?' He glanced at his watch. 'Half-past six. She may turn up at any minute.'

'I hope she does,' murmured Wedge.

'Well, if she doesn't, it'll look pretty fishy, you must admit,' said Lang.

'What is your case against Morris?'

'A pretty good one. In fact, I don't think even you can pick any holes in it! The first thing I looked for when I came into the case was a motive. Old Cartwright hadn't been robbed and, although the place had been broken into, it had been done by an amateur. It was your friend Walker who put me on to Morris, and I'm very grateful to him.'

'Anything ter oblige, mate, that's me all over . . .'

'Inquiries showed he and his uncle had been on bad terms for several weeks past,' went on Lang. 'The trouble was over this girl Helen Ford. The old man was dead against Morris having anything to do with her. Said her father was a bad lot, and most likely the girl was tarred with the same brush. They quarrelled violently on several occasions, and a customer who was in the shop during one of the rows came forward and stated he heard Morris threaten to kill Cartwright. I questioned Morris, and his behaviour was certainly suspicious. He admitted he and his uncle had quarrelled over the girl, and one day he'd lost his temper and told the old man if he didn't stop abusing the girl it would be the worse for him. But he swore he hadn't seen his uncle since then.'

He paused, but Inspector Wedge made no remark, and so he proceeded:

'Morris was unable to account for his movements during the time the murder was committed. At first he said he was in bed. But his landlady, who luckily was awake with the toothache, said he didn't come in until three. Then he changed his story and said he was worried because he'd got the sack — he'd been employed at Harpers', the cardboard box manufacturers — and had walked about trying to think what he should do about another job. His answers were so unsatisfactory I detained him for further inquiries, and very soon found I'd been wise. Harpers' gave him anything but a good character. They said he was lazy, and unreliable. Always trying to make money gambling instead of concentrating on his work. He owed a lot to his fellow-workers in the firm, and a lot more outside. In fact, his financial affairs were pretty bad, due mostly to gambling. Then we searched his room, and that clinched matters. We found a letter from his uncle asking him to come round to the shop at half-past twelve on the night the old man was killed. Wanted to see him urgently, he said. When we showed him the letter, Morris admitted receiving it. But he declared he hadn't gone, because he thought his uncle only wanted to start the old argument about his girl all over again.'

Lang paused and took a deep breath.

'That's the case against Morris,' he said. 'And when I tell you that in addition we discovered old Cartwright was worth a lot of money, and his will left everything to Morris, you must agree it's a very strong one.'

Wedge did agree, and said so. 'All the same,' he added, 'it's not conclusive. I've come up against circumstantial evidence just as strong, on more than one occasion, but which proved capable of an innocent explanation. For instance, in this case, it's quite possible Morris is telling nothing but the bare truth.'

' 'S'right,' Mr. Walker agreed.

Lang shook his head.

'What I refuse to do is to accept a surface explanation until it has been proved that there's no other,' Wedge pursued. 'The simple explanation for Ford's death was that he'd committed suicide. But by not accepting that until it had been proved, I discovered he'd been murdered.'

Further argument on the subject was stopped by the arrival of the ambulance.

The body of Ford was searched, but nothing of importance to the inquiry was found in any of his pockets. He was placed on a stretcher by the ambulance men, and carried out.

'By the way,' said Wedge, as the little divisional-surgeon was taking his departure, 'there'll be a post-mortem, of course. Will you particularly look for a blow on the head, or some form of drug that would have rendered him unconscious?'

For an instant the doctor looked surprised, and then his face cleared.

'Oh, yes, of course,' he replied. 'Something of the sort must have been administered to have got him to lie there quiet until the gas had done its work. Yes, I'll make a point of that.'

When he had gone, Inspector Lang and Wedge, watched by the interested Mr. Walker, made a search of the house. They found nothing until they came to the dead man's bedroom. Then Lang, who was rummaging in a drawer of an old dressing table, suddenly uttered an exclamation and looked up.

'What is it?' asked Wedge, turning round from an open cupboard.

'This!' exclaimed the other triumphantly, and held up a revolver. 'Look at it! It's been fired recently, and I'll bet the bullet found in old Cartwright's head will fit it. *Now* what about my theory? Doesn't this prove Morris and the girl were in it together?'

Mr. Walker looked at Wedge hopeful for a counter suggestion.

'It doesn't prove it,' came the answer, 'But it certainly points to it. However, perhaps we ought to wait until we've seen the girl and listened to what she has to say, before we jump to conclusions.'

But Helen Ford did not come home, although they waited for her until long past midnight. Neither had she come home when dawn broke greyly, revealing Pelham Street in all its dreary ugliness. She had, apparently, taken unto herself wings and vanished.

6

Mr. Walker wonders

An 'all-stations' call was sent out from
Scotland Yard, with a description of
Helen Ford. Every patrolling policeman
was warned to watch for her. A
photograph that had been found at her
home was produced in 'Printed Information' — one of the special newspapers
published by Scotland Yard, and not
available to the general public — and
circulated throughout the country. All
railway stations and ports of embarkation
were watched. But no information concerning the missing girl came to hand.
After her interview with Mr. Walker in the
café, she had completely disappeared.

Inspector Wedge got in touch with the
river police, and instructions were issued
to all patrol launches to keep a vigilant
watch up and down the river. There was
the bare possibility she might have

contemplated suicide.

It was about ten o'clock when Inspector Wedge and Mr. Walker ate a hearty breakfast together, after which the junkman set off for his home and a much-needed rest.

He lived in a little cul-de-sac off the Commercial Road, in a tiny house that stood next to a wood-yard. At the back was a shed, approached by a side-entrance, in which he kept his barrow and such of his stock-in-trade as was not readily disposable. In course of time this shed had become rather overcrowded, so there was just room for the barrow and that was all. Mr. Walker reached his abode with a sigh of thankfulness. His sleepless night on the top of a hard day had tired him out. He unlocked the door of the shed, put away his barrow, relocked the door, and entered the house through the kitchen. He lived entirely alone.

Taking off his coat and hat, he filled the kettle and put it on the gas stove. While it was boiling he had a wash in the sink, and then made himself a cup of tea, which he drank gratefully. And then he went to bed, falling asleep almost at once, and not waking until nearly five o'clock, when he got up, washed and dressed himself, and proceeded to set about cooking half a pound of sausages which should have formed last night's supper.

When these had been eaten he put a match to the fire in his little parlour, drew up an ancient chair, and lighting his pipe, settled down with great content, refreshed both bodily and mentally.

Well, he had bumped up against a queer business this time, he thought, as he watched the fire burn up. Mr. Walker puffed at his pipe and screwed up his face in perplexity. Not for a moment did he even consider Lang's theory as possible. Helen Ford wasn't the type of girl to be mixed up in a murder — at least, not in that way. And he was pretty sure she'd been speaking the truth when she'd told him her story in the café. She'd been genuinely worried to know what to do . . . Perhaps that was it. Perhaps she'd gone off somewhere to make up her mind.

It was a real teaser, and no mistake.

Who'd pushed old Ford's head in the gas oven? It had been pretty smart of Wedge to find that out, but who'd done it? The same person who'd killed old Cartwright?

'Lumme!' muttered Mr. Walker, expressing his thoughts aloud. 'If the same feller wot killed old Cartwright killed Ford, then it can't be Morris, 'cause 'e was in jug. An' if Ford was murdered instead o' committin' suicide, then it don't look as if 'e could 'ave killed Cartwright, in spite o' that there gun bein' found in 'is bedroom. An' if neither of 'em done 'im in, then 'oo blinkin' well did?'

He could not answer this question, so he propounded some more. Why'd old Cartwright sent that letter to Morris, asking him to go and see him at the shop, and why'd he chosen such a funny time? What'd he been doing there himself at half past twelve at night? The shop was shut in the normal way at eight, and it was a lock-up shop. What'd brought old Cartwright there so late? If he'd wanted to see his nephew so urgently, why couldn't he have seen him at his home and, again, why half past twelve?

It looked very much as if the old man had been up to some funny business.

Mr. Walker sat and pondered over these unanswerable questions until seven o'clock, when he put on his hat and coat and went round to the local pub for a glass of beer. Here he ran into some friends, and he was persuaded to join a foursome at darts, so it was fairly late before he got back home. Although he had slept for several hours during the day, habit asserted itself at his usual bedtime and he began to feel tired. But when he finally got to bed, sleep refused to come.

He lay staring into the darkness of his room, as wakeful as at noon. Eleven. Twelve. One. He heard the clock in the church near by strike every hour and, instead of his senses becoming dulled, they became more alert. A little while after the clock had struck one he heard the whine of a car. The sound reached him very plainly and then suddenly ceased. The car had stopped somewhere near at hand. Mr. Walker was vaguely curious. Cars were few and far between in that district at such an hour. He turned over on his other side, his bed creaking at the heavy movement, and listened, expecting to hear the car go on again, but there was no further sound. He closed his eyes, deliberately trying to make his mind a blank, but his thoughts would persist in churning round in his brain, in spite of all his efforts. He twisted over again and, in the act of doing so, suddenly became aware of a sound from the backyard below. It was the faintest of faint noises, but it was clearly audible in the stillness — the clink of metal against metal!

Mr. Walker hoisted himself out of bed and felt around in the darkness with his feet for his carpet slippers. He found them, thrust his feet into them, and shuffled over to the window. As he peered down into the backyard he saw a flash of light near the shed and discovered it came from a dark figure that was directing the dim ray of a torch on the lock. Mr. Walker drew in his breath with a slight hiss. Somebody was in his yard who'd no right to be there! Surely it couldn't be a burglar? The shed only contained his barrow and a mass of old junk, and everybody in the district knew it.

He left the window and hastily pulled on his trousers and jacket over his voluminous nightshirt. If it was a burglar, he was going to get a surprise. Opening the door, he cautiously made his way down the narrow stairs, along the passage, and into the kitchen. The back door was locked and chained, but, without making a sound, he unfastened the chain and turned the key.

The cold air of the night blew in as he opened the door carefully and peeped out. He had no wish to disturb the night prowler before he had a chance to see what he was like and, if possible, find out what his game was. So he took every precaution not to make any noise that might alarm him. He could see now it was a man in a long coat and cap. By the light of the torch he carried he was working on the padlock that secured the shed door. Mr. Walker, his round face set in grim lines, watched him.

The padlock was a good one and, hampered by having to hold the torch, the intruder seemed to be making slow progress. He succeeded at last, however, and gave a faint grunt of satisfaction as the spring catch clicked back.

Mr. Walker concluded the time had come to interrupt him. As silently as he could, he tiptoed through the door. He might have taken the other by surprise if he hadn't trodden on a loose stone, which ricked his ankle and forced a gasp of pain from him.

The man at the shed door swung round and his torch went out. Mr. Walker hobbled a few steps towards him, but he turned and ran for the side entrance. A moment later he could hear the man's flying footsteps fading away down the street. It was useless attempting to chase him. Even without an injured ankle, running was not one of Mr. Walker's strong points. He swore under his breath as he went to examine the damage that the man had done to the padlock. And then he heard the hum of a starting car engine. It grew louder and then died away in the distance. His lips pursed up, and very softly he whistled. So his unknown visitor had come and gone in a car. Very queer for someone to come in a car in order to rob a shed that contained nothing but junk.

The padlock was undamaged and, shutting it, Mr. Walker turned and limped, scratching his head thoughtfully, back into the house.

'And wot was all that about?' he muttered to himself. 'That's wot I wants ter know!'

7

The disappearance of Helen Ford

It was Helen Ford's intention when she left the café after her interview with Mr. Walker to go straight to Lucille's. She had just time to get there by ten o'clock if she hurried. She crossed the road, and began to walk quickly along towards the shop, unaware that the man who had come into the café as Mr. Walker left and followed her out, had got into a car that was waiting at the kerb and was now moving slowly along in her wake.

The first intimation she had of his presence was when the car drew up a few yards in front of her, and he got out, waiting for her to come level with him.

'Excuse me, miss — '

She stopped as he spoke, a little startled.

'You're Miss Ford, aren't you?' he went on, and when she nodded; 'I thought you were. I'm glad I saw you, it'll save me going to your house. I'm from the police, and I've been sent to take you to the station.' The sudden alarm she felt must have shown in her face, for he continued quickly: 'There's nothing to be scared about, miss. They just want you to confirm a statement Morris has made. Will you get in the car?'

He held open the door, but she hesitated.

'Couldn't I call at the place where I work?' she asked. 'If I come with you it will make me late, and they're rather particular about being in on time. It's only a little way up the street.'

'It's rather urgent,' he said. 'The detective is waiting to go out. Have they got a 'phone at the place where you work?'

She nodded.

'Well, that'll be all right, then,' he said quickly. 'You can phone from the station.'

Without further demur she stepped into the car, and he leaned through the door to wrap a rug around her knees. She felt a slight prick in her leg and uttered an exclamation.

'I'm sorry,' he said apologetically. 'There's a pin in this rug. Hope I didn't hurt you?'

She shook her head. Closing the door, he slid in behind the wheel, and the car moved forward. Her left leg felt numb where the pin had pricked her, and she rubbed it gently, while she wondered what statement Roy Morris could have made which required her confirmation, and why the matter was so urgent. And then she began to feel dizzy and faint. The passing street swam before her eyes, and the back of the man who was driving her grew hazy through the glass. She leaned forward to try to attract his attention, and everything went black.

★   ★   ★

Helen Ford came to herself feeling horribly sick, and with a splitting headache. The inside of her skull seemed as though it had been tightly packed with cotton wool.

As the dullness faded out of her brain she became aware that she was sitting in a chair. The reason why she felt so uncomfortable was because her arms and legs were tightly bound, with her wrists fastened by another rope to the back of the chair.

Still too dazed to be really alarmed, but sufficiently sensible to realise something was wrong, she raised her throbbing head and looked about her.

She was in a small room that was practically empty of furniture, and what little there was old and broken. A dirty window supplied the dim light that enabled her to see this, and facing it was a closed door. There was no carpet on the floor, but a ragged strip of linoleum covered a portion of the bare boards.

She tried to blink away the pain behind her eyes and concentrate her thoughts. Where was Mr. Walker? No, that was before she had met the man in the car . . . The man in the car was taking her to the police station . . . But this couldn't be the police station. What had happened? She had gone faint, and tried to attract his attention. Then blackness had descended suddenly and swiftly. She must have been taken ill, but — this wasn't a hospital. They didn't tie people to chairs in hospitals — neither did the police . . .

And then quite suddenly her mind cleared of all the mists that had enveloped it. The man in the car hadn't been from the police. His story had only been a trick to get her — here! For the first time a wave of fear swept over her. Who was he? Had her father discovered she knew, and — ? She dismissed that idea almost before it had completely formed in her mind. Her father would never do anything to harm her, whatever he might do to anyone else, and he couldn't be aware she knew. She had said nothing of what she had seen that night. He had no suspicion she had followed him to the old jeweller's and seen him climb the wall into the yard at the back of the shop. No suspicion she had watched him return, white-faced and shaking. But if it wasn't her father who had brought her to this place, wherever it was, who was it? Who else could have any reason?

The pain in her head was growing less,

and the throbbing was diminishing, but with the cessation of one pain she became more acutely conscious of another. The confining cords which bound her to the chair cut into her flesh, and the upright position in which she was forced to sit made her back ache. She tried to ease herself into a more comfortable position, but she had been tied too tightly.

She wondered how long it was since she had got into the car in the Commercial Road, but she could not see the tiny wristwatch she wore, however much she tried, and had no means of telling.

Wherever she was it was very quiet. She could hear no sounds of passing traffic, nor even the distant rumble of it. Presently, after a long lapse of time, she did hear a sound — the noise of a car somewhere outside. It stopped, and then there was silence again until a door shut in the house below her, and a footstep sounded on an uncarpeted stair. A heavy tread came as far as the door of the room in which she sat, and, after a pause, a key rasped in the lock.

She caught her breath, and her eyes fixed themselves on the door as it slowly opened. The man who had spoken to her in the Commercial Road came quietly into the room. He pressed down the light switch beside the door, which turned on a small lamp that stood close to the girl's chair.

He was still dressed in the heavy overcoat he had worn when she had first seen him, and the soft-brimmed felt hat. He said nothing, but stood looking at her, and there was something in this silent scrutiny that terrified her. The flood of angry questions in her brain would not form into words. Dry-mouthed, her heart thudding until she thought she would suffocate, she could only stare at him in breathless fear.

She had taken little notice of him before, but now she noticed a small black moustache shaded his upper lip. There was something vaguely familiar about him. It seemed to her she had either seen or met him somewhere, but she couldn't think where.

After a little while he came over to her

chair and tested the chords at her ankles, wrists, and arms. As a further precaution, he tied a handkerchief over her mouth. He completed these actions without speaking a word. And then, as quietly as he had arrived, he left, locking the door behind him.

8

Inspector Wedge has a theory

Sergeant Matthews faced Inspector Wedge across the latter's desk in his office at Scotland Yard.

'There's no news of the girl at all,' he was saying. 'Can't understand it. She's given us the slip somehow.'

It was the morning following the day of the search for Helen Ford that had continued — without success. Wedge had now officially taken charge of the Shop Murder Case, as the newspapers headlined it, and was listening to his sergeant's report of the progress so far.

'It looks like we'll have to let Morris go, too, doesn't it?' the sergeant said.

Wedge nodded, and watched a ring of smoke from his cigarette in its long holder rise towards the ceiling. Two men had come forward and provided Morris with what seemed to be a watertight alibi.

They had been working on some repairs to the tramlines about a mile and a half away from Cartwright's shop. They said that just after it had struck midnight Morris had come along and stood watching them for about ten minutes. They both swore it was he — they could see him quite distinctly by the light of the acetylene flares which they were using for their work.

Both men knew him quite well because they lived in the same street and had often met him at the same public house. They stated that after he had got tired of watching them Morris had moved off in the opposite direction from the shop. Just as they had finished their work which was about half past two, he had passed them coming back. The jeweller, according to the doctor, was killed after one and before three, and Morris could not have been in two places at once.

'Of course,' murmured Wedge, thinking aloud, 'the alibi isn't absolutely conclusive. He could have gone back to the shop by some other route, shot Cartwright, and returned by the same way in order to pass these men and establish an alibi.'

The inspector passed his hand over his thinning hair. 'The only thing,' he said, speaking through a cloud of cigarette smoke, 'is that if he'd done that it would've been natural for him to have mentioned these men since the whole object was they should see him.'

'Unless we could prove he came back by another route,' ventured Matthews, 'those fellows' evidence would go a long way with the jury, don't you agree?'

The other nodded. 'You know I don't think this case is nearly so simple as it looks on paper. For instance, there was no sign of a struggle having taken place between Cartwright and his murderer.'

'That's true.'

'And yet,' murmured Wedge, 'the shop was broken into. Doesn't that strike you as queer? Here is a man in a shop full of valuable property. It is at an unusual hour and yet he allows someone to break in without apparently making any effort to stop them.'

'He was expecting Morris — ' suggested

Matthews. But the inspector interrupted him.

'But he wasn't expecting him to break in. He wrote asking Morris to come and see him at half past twelve. If he'd heard a sound at the back door he would have been suspicious at once for Morris would naturally come to the front of the shop. There is no way round to the back except by climbing a wall into the yard. A man who has come by invitation is hardly likely to go to that trouble when he only has to tap on the front door to be admitted.'

'The appearance of the place having been broken into might have been done after the murder as a blind.'

'Which means,' replied Wedge quietly, 'that the murderer was admitted by Cartwright. Therefore the jeweller knew him. Knew him so well in fact, that he let him in at that late hour with no misgiving.'

'Which is just what he'd do in the case of Morris,' said Matthews.

'Quite,' agreed the other. 'But Morris said he didn't go. Let's take it that he didn't. In that case the person who did was somebody else. Now, did this somebody else know Cartwright was expecting Morris? Or did he just see a light in the shop and knock? Or had the jeweller arranged an appointment with him as well?'

The sergeant leant forward. 'What about this?' he said. 'Cartwright was dead against this engagement between Morris and the girl, wasn't he?'

Inspector Wedge nodded.

'Well, he writes a note to Morris, asking him to call, and he also writes to the girl. The man doesn't go, but the girl does. The old man says what he thinks to her. She loses her temper and shoots him. Then she tries to make it look as though someone had broken in. Her boy friend is arrested for the murder and to get him off she thinks up this cock-and-bull story about her father just as I said. Doesn't that fit? Cartwright would've let her in because he was expecting her — '

'It fits in essentials,' murmured Wedge. 'But the detail's all wrong. Either you've got to assume she went with the idea of killing Cartwright, or she actually carries a revolver about with her. The latter is rubbish, and the former is little better.'

The sergeant sighed ruefully as he saw his idea being exploded by his superior's icy logic.

'Why should she go with the intention of killing the old man?' pursued Wedge. 'Morris had refused to listen to him, he was prepared to stick to her. Cartwright couldn't harm her in any way. No. It sounds all right, Matthews, but I don't think it is right.'

He gave the sergeant a little smile and proceeded.

'If the jeweller had wanted to see these two together why choose that time of night? You know to my mind, that's the crux of the whole affair. Why did Cartwright go to the shop at such a late hour, and why did he want Morris to meet him there?'

He wagged his cigarette holder in emphasis of his precisely uttered words.

'You think, and Morris thought so too, it was to continue to press his objections to the engagement but is that so? He could've done that at any time without choosing the middle of the night.'

Inspector Wedge returned the holder to its place between his teeth and leaned back in his chair.

'Find out why he went to the shop at midnight,' he said, 'why he wanted Morris there, and you've solved the mystery.'

Sergeant Matthews shifted restlessly in his chair 'The only thing is,' he pointed out, 'if the girl isn't in this — and pretty deep — why's she disappeared?'

'I know. Helen Ford's vanishing trick doesn't fit the puzzle at all. You see, if your theory was right about her, the very last thing she'd do would be to disappear like this.'

The sergeant nodded.

'She goes to a whole lot of trouble and risk to lay the blame on her father,' the inspector pursued, 'and then deliberately throws it all overboard by running away.'

'Perhaps,' said Matthews, 'what happened was that she got up to a certain point and then just panicked — '

'But anyone who could plan sheer

cold-blooded murder, as you're suggesting she did,' interrupted Wedge impatiently, '*wouldn't* panic. That's the point.'

The sergeant, a little uncomfortable, could only answer with a query. 'Then what's happened to her? If she hasn't run away, what's she done?'

'Supposing,' Wedge said, 'somebody *wanted* you to think just what you've thought? Somebody *wanted* to make it look as though Helen Ford was guilty of both murders? Wouldn't it be to their advantage to arrange for her not to be in a position to defend herself?'

Sergeant Matthews sat up abruptly. 'Good Lord!' he exclaimed, 'you mean —?'

'I mean,' murmured Wedge, 'there is an alternative to Helen Ford having disappeared of her own free will. And the alternative is that she was forced to go by the real murderer of Cartwright and her father.'

9

The secret of the junk shed

There followed a short silence while Sergeant Matthews digested the other's words. It was broken by the telephone burring at Wedge's elbow. He answered it, and his eyes twinkled as he listened.

'Right,' he said, 'show him up,' and he replaced the receiver. The sergeant now found his voice.

'D'you really think the girl is being kept hidden away somewhere? I can't help feeling the girl has just done a bunk — '

Matthews was interrupted by the arrival of Mr. Walker, who was shown into the room by an officer. The junkman was limping, but his smile was as cheery as ever.

'Good mornin', chums,' he grinned.

The officer who had shown him in withdrew, and the inspector greeted Mr. Walker and introduced him to Sergeant Matthews.

'Sit down, Walker,' Wedge waved him to a chair. 'Been no news about Miss Ford, I'm afraid.'

Mr. Walker's genial face clouded as he carefully lowered his ponderous bulk into the chair and sat down. 'No news at all, eh? Looks bad ter me, mate. Where can she 'ave got to?'

'That's what we'd like to know,' said the sergeant heartily. 'The inspector here has the idea she's been kidnapped or something — '

'Well, now, mate,' interrupted Mr. Walker. 'I shouldn't wonder at it, neither. 'T'ain't likely she'd 'ave 'ad much money, an' you'd 'ave 'eard somethink of her by now if she'd just 'opped it like.'

Sergeant Matthews rose. 'Well, anyway, I'll be getting on with some checking up, eh?'

Wedge inclined his head, and with a nod to the junkman, the sergeant quitted the office. Mr. Walker watched him go, then turned to his friend.

'Don't 'e think a lot o' your idea, chum?' he winked.

'I'm afraid Sergeant Matthews lacks

imagination,' murmured the detective. 'And, of course, I may be quite wrong. How did you manage to hurt your foot?'

Mr. Walker extended his right leg and regarded his ungainly boot with a frown.

In his slow, rather ponderous way, he related his adventure of the previous night. Wedge listened interestedly.

'You seem to attract unusual problems like a magnet,' he smiled, when the junkman had finished. 'Is there anything of value in this shed of yours?'

'Nothink as valuable as that,' replied Mr. Walker. 'It's worth a bit ter me, some of it. Some of it ain't worth nothink. But there ain't nothink there worth goin' ter the trouble o' breakin' in.'

'The man who tried must have thought there was, or he wouldn't have taken the risk. Perhaps among some of the stuff you've bought there is something valuable that got in by accident.'

'Well, it'll be the first time,' said Mr. Walker, his big face breaking into a broad grin. 'I always used ter wonder whether old Cartwright mightn't 'ave chucked away some jools in the stuff 'e give me ter cart away, but — '

'Did you buy stuff from him?' cut in the inspector sharply.

'Well, more often than not 'e used ter give it me. It was nothink much as a rule — mostly rubbish — '

'Are you very busy today?

'Takin' the day orf, I am, on account o' me foot,' Mr. Walker explained. ' 'T'ain't exac'ly 'urtin' me, but I couldn't do me usual round, pushin' the old barrer — '

'I'd like to have a look at this shed of yours,' said Wedge, getting up suddenly and fitting a fresh cigarette into his holder. 'Any objection if we run down there now?'

'Anythink ter oblige, chum, that's me all over,' responded Mr. Walker cheerfully. 'Though I don't reckon as 'ow yer'll find anythink there worth the trouble.'

'I'll risk that. When did you last take a consignment of junk from Cartwright's?'

'Must've bin two days afore the murder I took the larst lot. 'Ere, you don't think that feller wot come larst night 'ad anythink ter do with killin' the old bloke, do yer?'

'I don't think anything at the moment,' replied Wedge. 'But the fact that somebody tried to break into your shed, and came in a car to do it, is sufficiently extraordinary to make me curious.'

★ ★ ★

Inspector Wedge was very silent as, accompanied by Mr. Walker, he drove in a fast car towards Commercial Road. There might be nothing in his idea — after all, it was a very long shot. But he had taken long shots before, and now and again they had come off. Was there any connection between this attempt to break into Mr. Walker's shed and the murder of Cartwright?

On the face of it, it seemed unlikely, but Mr. Walker had been in the habit of getting junk from the old jeweller. He had taken away a consignment two days before the murder, and this attempt to break into his shed had occurred a few days after. And the man had come in a car, which argued he had known what he was about. It had been no little sneak thief just taking potluck on the off chance of picking up something on which he might raise a little cash.

Under Mr. Walker's instructions, the detective-inspector found the little cul-de-sac and brought the car to a stop outside his small house. The junkman got heavily out and escorted his companion to the side entrance, and round into the yard at the back.

The shed was a large building of tarred wood, which occupied most of the available space. Mr. Walker unlocked the padlock that secured the door, pulling it wide.

' 'Ere's the scene o' the crime, mate,' he said. 'Mind 'ow you go. There ain't a lot o' room.'

There wasn't. The interior of the shed was packed with all sorts and conditions of things. Broken pieces of furniture, old motor tyres, rusty bits of bicycles, bedsteads, ancient suitcases, and trunks. In one corner was a stack of old fenders, and in another a pile of pots and pans. The whole place was crammed with junk of every conceivable description.

From the open doorway, the inspector surveyed the untidy collection rather ruefully. It would take hours to go through that heap of rubbish thoroughly.

'Have you any idea where you put this last lot of stuff you got from Cartwright's?' he asked.

'Can't say as 'ow I 'ave, chum,' Mr. Walker declared candidly. 'Yer see, I usually kind o' sorts it over when I buys it, an' clears it orf the old barrer when I comes in, so's it'll be ready in the mornin'. Then every now an' ag'in I 'as a clear-out like, an' sells wot's any good.'

'I see. Well, do you think we could move the barrow out? That would give a little more room.'

Mr. Walker agreed to this suggestion, and pulled that aged contraption into the light of day. Wedge stepped into the shed and inspected its contents at closer quarters.

'Would you remember the things from Cartwright's when we come across them?' he said as Mr. Walker joined him. The junkman nodded.

'Then we'll make a start.'

And, taking off his overcoat, Wedge draped it over a marble-topped wash-stand, minus one leg.

It was an even more difficult task than he had anticipated. But by working methodically, and with Mr. Walker's assistance, he gradually made headway.

After clearing one side of the shed they paused for a rest.

'Well, chum,' gasped Mr. Walker, wiping his streaming face with a gaily coloured handkerchief, 'there ain't noth-ink in that lot wot's worth burglin'.'

'And quite a lot that I shouldn't think you want,' said Wedge. 'Come on! Let's tackle the rest.'

Almost as soon as they started, he came upon a battered jewel-case, and held it up. 'This looks as though it might have come from Cartwright's,' he said.

Mr. Walker looked at it, and nodded. 'Yes, I remembers that, mate,' he replied. 'It's empty, though. There was two more empty ones — '

'They're here!' broke in the detective, stooping, 'and empty, as you say. This is probably where you put the junk from Cartwright's when you cleared it off the barrow.'

Mr. Walker confirmed this supposition when he had examined the heap on which the inspector had found the jewel-cases. It was a heterogeneous collection of odds and ends. Among the whole assortment there was nothing of any real value.

'Is that the lot?' asked Wedge, throwing down a scratched mahogany box after he had discovered to his disappointment it was empty. 'Was there anything else from Cartwright's?'

'Dunno as 'ow I rec'lects anythink else,' Mr. Walker answered.

Inspector Wedge frowned. Apparently his long shot wasn't coming off this time. There was nothing here that anyone would even bother to pick up if it was lying in the gutter, much less risk attempted burglary to get it. If there was anything of value it must be amongst the rest of the stuff. That meant the man who had come in the night had nothing to do with the old jeweller's murder, after all.

His method of going through the various objects in the shed was to arrange them in a series of neat piles, examining each separately as he did so. He was proceeding to continue this with the next batch when he caught sight of a whitish object lying on the floor. It was behind the heap he had just dealt with, and lay close up against the wall.

Stepping carefully over things in his way, he reached down and picked it up. It was a piece of cloth that had once been white, but was now a dirty grey. He could tell by its weight there was something knotted up in the folds. He brought his find out into a better light. It was a handkerchief, the four corners of which had been tied together to form a sort of bag.

'Wot yer got 'old of there, chum?' asked Mr. Walker, straightening up from trying to shift a heavy box of old books.

'I don't know, but it looks the most interesting thing I've come across yet.' Wedge was busily untying the knots.

'Now, where did that come from?' muttered Mr. Walker. 'I don't remember seein' that there afore . . . Lor luv-a-duck! Look at that!'

From the untied handkerchief had suddenly leapt a blaze of scintillating fire.

'That's what your visitor of the night came for,' murmured Inspector Wedge.

On the handkerchief in his palm lay a diamond necklace!

10

Inspector Wedge sets a trap

Inspector Wedge and Mr. Walker hurried back to Scotland Yard, and the detective left the junkman in his office while he pursued certain enquiries regarding the diamond necklace.

This did not take him long, and presently he was back in his office to find Mr. Walker comfortably ensconced in a chair with a cigar and the evening paper.

'Well, you ain't bin gorn long, chum,' he greeted the inspector.

'Long enough to find out the history of your diamond necklace.'

'T'ain't mine, worse luck!' said Mr. Walker. 'But what I wants ter know is 'ow it come ter be in my shed.'

Wedge went over to his desk and leant back in his chair, the inevitable cigarette holder in his mouth.

'The necklace itself is the property of

Lady Glanore. It was stolen from her house in Morley Square, with a lot of other jewellery three weeks ago. The police were, and are, pretty certain who the thief was, but he managed to get out of the country before they could arrest him. He's quite a clever little burglar named Gale — Johnny Gale. Used to live at Camberwell Green, but, after the robbery at Lady Glanore's, when our friend Inspector Lang went to arrest him, he'd gone, and the stolen jewellery had gone with him.'

'Lumme! An 'ow did this 'ere necklace get inter my shed, mate?'

'I don't think it's very hard to answer that. You took it there in that lot of junk you got from Cartwright.'

'But I'd 've noticed it, chum. I'd 've seen it when I looked over the stuff.'

'When did you look over the stuff?' asked the detective. 'I'll hazard a guess that on this particular occasion you didn't look over what you'd got from Cartwright's.'

'Luv us, but you're right!' said Mr. Walker excitedly. 'Now I comes ter think of it, I didn't. I was in a bit of an 'urry that day — got an appointment I 'ad with a bloke wot 'ad a lot of old scrap iron 'e wanted ter git rid of, an 'scrap iron's a good sellin' line — but I looked it over when I got back — '

'If I'm right, the necklace in the handkerchief was put in that battered old mahogany box by the jeweller. He accidentally included the box in the stuff you took away.'

Mr. Walker's mouth remained open.

'When you put it on your barrow it fell out and got hidden among the sacking. You may have carried it about for several days without knowing it, and then eventually it dropped out in the shed and got hidden up among all the other litter. That's the only way I can account for your not knowing it was there.'

Mr. Walker gulped, closed his mouth and then opened it again.

'Lumme! Fancy me a-pushing me old barrer about with them-there sparklers in it an' not knowin' it! But 'ow did they get into old Cartwright's 'ands?'

'That's a little bit more complicated. I

think I can answer it, but I'd rather not just at the moment. I want to be quite sure first.'

'When'll that be, mate?'

'Well, with your co-operation, I hope it will be tonight. The man who came after that necklace last night doesn't know it's been found yet. But he also doesn't know how long it will be before it is. Therefore he's got no time to waste. I think he'll make another attempt to get it tonight, and if he does, we'll be waiting for him.

'I get yer, chum. An' I'll bet yer I can put a name ter the bloke wot'll come — this feller wotcher jest bein talkin' about,' said Mr. Walker shrewdly. 'Johnny Gale.'

'Well, we shall see if you're right. I'll tell you one thing though, that handkerchief the necklace was wrapped in was neither Gale's nor Cartwright's.'

It had come on to rain when Inspector Wedge and Mr. Walker left Scotland Yard. The pavements and roadways were streaming with water as they sped towards the City.

Sergeant Matthews was at the wheel,

and nosed the black car expertly through the traffic until in due course they reached a garage in the Commercial Road. Wedge informed the other two that from here they would have to walk.

'Look at the rain!' muttered the sergeant.

'A spot of rain won't hurt you!' replied the inspector. 'I have no desire to advertise our presence. It's not far, and you can turn your collars up.'

Wedge's optimistic remarks about the rain, however, were hardly justified, for when they arrived at Mr. Walker's house the water was pouring from them, and their shoes squelched unpleasantly at every step.

'Come on in, chums, an' get yer coats orf,' came the husky voice of Mr. Walker, as he succeeded at last in turning the key, which had been a little stiff. 'There's worse things wot 'appens at sea!'

'There can't be much more water, anyhow!' snorted Sergeant Matthews dragging his sodden overcoat from his back and thrusting it truculently at the hook which Mr. Walker pointed out.

'I'll 'ave the fire goin' in 'alf a shake,' said the junkman, pushing open the door of his little parlour. 'An' then we'll be all nice an' cosy-like.'

Half an hour later they were sitting round a blazing fire listening to the noise of the rain as it hissed and splashed outside.

11

Mr. Walker learns the truth

It was at twelve o'clock when Wedge suggested they should begin the serious part of the vigil. Rather reluctantly, they followed him out to the shed.

'You two go inside,' said the detective when Mr. Walker had opened the door and wheeled his 'barrer' outside and round the side of the house to make room.

'I'll join you in a minute,' he went on. 'Afraid I shall have to damage your property slightly, Walker, but I'll make it good.'

'Orl right, chum.'

'I'm going to lock you both inside,' said Wedge. 'Can't afford to leave the place unlocked. Might frighten our man away.'

They squeezed themselves into the shed, and the detective closed the door and fastened the padlock. Then, going round to the side, he took a large chisel, with which he had thoughtfully come provided, from his pocket and prised loose two of the planks. There was just sufficient room for him to wriggle his long and narrow form through, and he pulled the boards as well as he could back into position.

'There we are!' he said. 'Now there's nothing we can do except wait. I'm afraid we can't smoke,' he added — and there was a distinctly mournful note in his voice — 'he might smell it.'

They waited in the darkness perched on various oddments of Mr. Walker's stock-in-trade, and the passing time seemed endless. The rain beat down relentlessly, drumming on the roof so that the shed was filled with noise. It drowned every outside sound, and the first intimation they had that their watch was ended was the rattle of the padlock. The inspector heard Mr. Walker draw in a quick breath and then gently let it come hissing through his teeth. Matthew's rather heavy breathing stopped abruptly, and there was the faintest rustle as he stiffened involuntarily.

Three pairs of eyes strained through the darkness in the direction of the door as the three men waited motionless for the moment when it should open.

It came at last. There was the scrape of metal against metal as the padlock was removed from the staples, and then the creak of a hinge. The door was pulled open. A ray of light split the blackness and went, dancing about over the various objects with which the place was filled.

Behind the torch, dimly visible in the reflected light appeared the shadowy figure of a man. He advanced cautiously, step by step and inch by inch, picking his way carefully over the littered floor and sweeping his light from side to side.

He was scarcely a yard away when Wedge straightened up.

★   ★   ★

It was some time later, in Inspector Wedge's office, and Mr. Walker was saying to the detective:

'I'm still a bit 'azy as ter the why and

100

the wherefore like of all this 'ere 'ow-d'yer-do — '

'Well,' said the other, 'it's very simple really. As you know, Johnny Gale got away with a lot of jewellery from Lady Glanore's house in the West End. The police were pretty sure he was the burglar because the job was stamped with his methods. Lang was sent to question him. He'd been a crook ever since he joined the police force, though he was clever enough not to be found out until now, and he agreed to let Gale get away in exchange for the necklace.

'Lang, being smart, didn't attempt to sell the necklace to a fence. He knew in the first place he'd get very little for it. Secondly, fences are a dangerous breed, are apt to turn informers on the slightest provocation. He adopted a better plan. He went to an elderly short-sighted, but honest jeweller in his own division. His idea was that if the jeweller became suspicious about the diamonds being stolen property and notified the police, he in his capacity of inspector would be able to allay that suspicion.

'So he adopted a simple disguise and took the necklace to Cartwright. His story was that he wanted it reset as a bracelet. His wife had grown tired of it as it was or something of that sort. Later he could have said his wife didn't like it in its new form, and therefore he wanted to sell it. That is actually the story, he was going to use with Cartwright.'

'I gets yer, chum.'

'But all his plans were upset because the old man saw through his disguise. Or, rather, to be more accurate, he thought he had. He wasn't sure, but something about Lang in his character of the owner of the necklace reminded the jeweller of Lang the policeman. Not being sure, however, he didn't say anything. But he made an appointment with Lang to come and see him. He chose a time when the interview would be assured of privacy — because, you must remember, he still wasn't sure.'

The junkman nodded understandingly.

'As a safeguard he decided to ask his nephew, Morris, to be present. A witness to what might take place would be useful.

In the meanwhile a terrible thing happened from Cartwright's point of view. He couldn't find the necklace. He was under the impression he'd put it in the safe, but it wasn't there.'

Wedge paused to remove a used cigarette from his long holder, and insert a new one. Mr. Walker waited for him to continue with hardly concealed impatience as the detective applied a match to his cigarette and continued.

'Lang kept the appointment, taking the precaution to go armed because he guessed why the old man wanted to see him so secretly. Cartwright accused him of being the man who brought the necklace in to be reset, and to substantiate his accusation cited the fact that the handkerchief in which the piece of jewellery was wrapped bore his initials.'

'Lumme!' exclaimed Mr. Walker.

'Cartwright had to admit he hadn't got it. Lang thought he was trying to double-cross him, and although Cartwright swore he'd lost it, he wouldn't believe him. The old man said all he could think was the necklace had been accidentally taken away in some old rubbish he gave to a junkman. If that was the case, he told Lang, it would be all right, because Walker would return it as soon as he found it.'

The junkman nodded vigorously. ''S'right, chum — honesty's the best policy.

The inspector smiled. 'Lang still believed it was an excuse to do him out of the diamonds, and in his rage over this and because Cartwright knew too much, he shot him.'

'Lumme, chum, wot a proper 'ow-d'yer-do, ain't it?'

'That's only part of it,' continued the other. 'While Lang was searching for the necklace he heard a noise at the back door of the shop. Scared he would be found with the body of the old jeweller, he decided to clear out by the front entrance. But looking through the glass he saw Helen Ford standing in the shadow of the shop. He couldn't go out that way or she'd be bound to see him. There was only one thing to do, and he did it. He hid. Presently he saw old Ford come in through the back door. The old man spotted the body of Cartwright on the floor, and bolted for his life. Lang realised what had happened. Old Ford, who was a thoroughly bad lot, had come to burgle the place. His daughter had probably followed him — she was always trying to keep her father straight. The knowledge gave Lang a sudden idea, which he worked out in detail, for safeguarding himself. What that idea was and how he carried it out, you don't need me to tell you.'

'And 'e pinched the girl, eh?'

'Yes, for the same reason — to try to ensure no suspicion should fall on him,' answered the detective. 'She was found at an old cottage rented by Lang, in the country.'

'D'yer think,' — Mr. Walker leaned forward, his voice very low and hoarse. 'D'yer think 'e would 'ave done 'er in, too?'

'I should say nothing was more certain. If she'd been killed — and buried — both the murders might have been attributed to her.'

'Well, I s'pose that Morris feller is free

now, mate? 'E'll come inter the old man's money, an' then, o'course, 'e'll marry the girl.' Mr. Walker scratched his chin slowly. 'And ter think if I 'and't run inter 'er this 'ere chap Lang might've got away with it. Lang . . . now there's a queer bloke for yer and no blinkin' error. Fancy! A perlice-inspector and a crook as well. It don't seem possible as 'ow a man could carry on living two lives like that. Do it?'

'All the same he did. I suppose he found it a good way to swell his pay envelope and thought it worth the risk.'

'But you wouldn't think after 'avin' reached the position 'e 'ad 'e'd stoop to such dirty work?'

Wedge shrugged. 'Probably he'd got into financial difficulties or something of that sort. There are a number of reasons why a man in that position might use it to cloak dishonesty and crime. As you know he was a pretty tough individual and there was nothing he wouldn't stop at.'

'Yer mean the way 'e murdered them two?'

'Exactly.'

Mr. Walker shook his head sadly at this

106

glimpse of the dark and evil aspect of human nature. He was not exactly unaccustomed to coming into contact with all sorts of people, a number of whom he knew, or guessed, were of the underworld, or lived on the fringe of it. Nevertheless, although he had often found it in his heart to sympathise with many a crook — especially those whom he felt had never been given a decent start in life — the crime of murder was to him a terrible and almost inexcusable thing.

'Ah well,' he sighed, ' 'e can't do no more 'arm now.'

'No,' replied the other, 'Mr. Lang's two-sided career has come to a sticky end. He's got to pay the price for his cold-blooded killing . . . there'll be no escape for him from that.'

The detective blew a cloud of cigarette smoke ceilingwards. 'Yes, Mr. Walker,' he murmured as he lazily watched a smoke ring widen and dissolve, 'The case of the shop murder is closed, and our friend Lang's account is closed too.'

' 'S' right.'

Which was where Inspector Wedge and

Mr. Walker were wrong. The shop murder case had certainly been brought to an end in so far as the murderer had been unmasked. But the case of Lang, one time police inspector now revealed as a crook and killer, was far from closed.

Inspector Wedge was destined to find in him a far more cunning and dangerous adversary than he realised. And Mr. Walker was to make his acquaintance once more.

12

Mr. Walker buys an aspidistra

It was the following day, and Mr. Walker was shoving his old barrow along a street in Bloomsbury.

'Any old rags, bottles, or bones,' he called in his rich, fruity tones.

Slowly he trundled along. Mr. Walker, for once, was showing little interest in the passers-by who, attracted by his voice, stopped to smile at the junkman. His thoughts were still with Inspector Wedge and the extraordinary arrest of Lang.

Almost mechanically he continued to cry:

'Any old bones . . . Any old rags . . . '

It was the sound of his voice, as he approached her neat house, that caused Miss Tillington to turn to Miss Finchley, who stood beside her in the hall, the door of which was open, and remark:

'A rag and bone man, my dear. The

very person! Really, one would almost think providence had sent him on purpose.'

Miss Finchley smiled a watery smile. She occupied the first floor in her companion's house, and was what Miss Tillington genteelly described as a 'paying-guest.' She followed the other out of the front door and on to the pavement. Down the street they saw coming towards them a stout man of ruddy countenance pushing a laden barrow upon which was piled an indescribable quantity of junk.

'Any rags, bottles or bones,' called Mr. Walker and Miss Tillington beckoned to him peremptorily.

'Here! Here, my good man! I want you.'

Mr. Walker brought his thoughts back to the present, and the possible business in hand. Obligingly he brought his barrow to a halt at the kerb and turned a beaming face towards Miss Tillington.

'Wotcher, lady!' he said genially. 'Luv'ly day, ain't it?'

Miss Tillington, ignoring this social gambit as beneath her dignity, brought the conversation back to a strictly business basis.

'I have one or two articles for disposal,' she said in her high-pitched, querulous voice. 'I should be glad if you would look at them and make me an offer.'

'Anythink to oblige, lady,' said Mr. Walker cheerfully. 'That's me all over. Wotcher got?'

'If you will step inside, I will show you.'

'I really must be running along,' put in Miss Finchley hurriedly. She explained to the other about a tea party to which she was on her way. 'I shall be so late, and Lady Potter is so very strict about punctuality — quite rightly, of course — '

She lapsed into incoherence, murmured an almost inaudible 'good-bye' and tripped away. Mr. Walker shot a humorous glance after her and followed Miss Tillington into the house.

'These are the things,' said that lady, nodding at the heap in the hall, and Mr. Walker regarded the collection a little dubiously.

'Well, chum — ' he began, and was

instantly pulled up by the irate Miss Tillington.

'You will kindly refrain from familiarity, my good man,' she said coldly. 'When you address me you will do so respectfully, please.'

'Lumme!' thought Mr. Walker. 'Wot a lady! Anyone 'ud think she was the Grand Duchess of Timbuctoo to 'ear 'er talk, only if she was she'd be a bit more matey!'

Without answering, he made a closer inspection of the miscellaneous pile in the hall. There was nothing worth very much. A few chairs, none of them undamaged in some way. An old wooden bedstead and a roll of bedding. Three tables with stained tops and broken legs. A washstand with a tin basin. A battered leather trunk containing several articles of clothing, including two pairs of very worn boots. Two wooden boxes full of cheap crockery and ornaments, and a gaudily painted bowl containing an aspidistra in a pot. This last seemed to Mr. Walker to be the best of the bunch. He was rather partial to aspidistras — there were three of them in his sitting room, occupying a bamboo stand in the window — and this would fill a vacant shelf.

'That's a nice plant, mum,' he said, fingering the leaves. 'Gorn orf a bit, but a drop o' water an' a rub up'll soon put it right.'

Miss Tillington sniffed. She hated aspidistras: to her they represented bad taste and were a badge of the lower classes.

'I shall be glad if you would let me know what these things are worth to you, and remove them as quickly as possible.'

There was more than a trace of bitterness in Miss Tillington's voice as she gazed short-sightedly through her gold-rimmed pince-nez at the pile of oddments the delivery men had stacked in her neat hall earlier that day.

Indeed the arrival of the miscellaneous array of junk had come as a great shock to her to say nothing of filling her with disgust and dismay. When, on the death of her uncle, his solicitors had informed her of his houseful of furniture and belongings to which she was entitled,

Miss Tillington had expected something very different.

She had always understood her uncle to be in affluent circumstances. Even though he was a most eccentric man living entirely alone in a cottage on the wildest part of Dartmoor. He had died from what were apparently the results of a stroke, and had not been found until a week after.

There had been no will, but her hopes had been high when she had received the letter from her uncle's solicitors informing her she was the only living relative of the dead man, they had been able to trace. All of the eccentric Mr. Pringle's property would come to her, they wrote.

Secretly she had always believed this uncle, whom she had not seen since she was in her teens, was a very rich man, and one day she would inherit all his money. But her dreams had been shattered. There was no money. Only a miserable collection of broken furniture and bits and pieces that were worth very little.

These thoughts passed through her

mind while she waited for Mr. Walker to name his price.

After scratching his chin over the mental arithmetic involved, he gave her a figure. In spite of Miss Tillington's extreme gentility she was not above haggling over a bargain, however, and haggle she did.

Mr. Walker listened to all she had to say, interpolating, when he got the opportunity a few remarks of his own. Finally he shook his head.

'That's all wot they're worth ter me, lady. If yer wants more for 'em, you'll 'ave ter sell 'em ter someone else.'

Miss Tillington realised he meant what he said. Grudgingly she accepted. Money was passed from his podgy hands to her thin, predatory ones, and the legacy that her uncle had left her was transferred to Mr. Walker's barrow. He roped his new acquisitions carefully in place, finding a safe spot for the aspidistra, and moved cheerfully off.

As he trudged along his thoughts went back to the thin, bitter-faced female he had left behind. Idly he wondered how the articles she had owned, and which now reposed on his barrow, had come into her possession. Then his thoughts returned once again to the more interesting subject of the shop murder case and his friend Inspector Wedge.

He considered for a moment the idea of making the tall, long-faced detective a present of the aspidistra, but on second thoughts decided it would not appeal to him.

'Anyway,' he chuckled to himself, 'if I did give it 'im, 'e'd only suffocate it with 'is continual cigarette-smokin' wot 'e don't never seem to stop!'

Little did Mr. Walker realise as he turned his ambling footsteps towards home how coincidental had been the flow of his thoughts . . . From the woman in the Bloomsbury house, who had sold him the aspidistra, to his chum, Inspector Wedge . . . Had the junkman been asked at that time what connection had joined his thoughts about these two people, seemingly poles apart, he would have answered that there was none.

But he would have been wrong.

That aspidistra, seemingly an innocent-looking plant that was now perched on his barrow, and which he even considered presenting to Inspector Wedge as a gift — how was he to forsee it was to throw him and the Scotland Yard detective together again in extraordinary circumstances?

And in only a few hours' time . . .

Meanwhile, in his office at Scotland Yard, Inspector Wedge was answering the urgent summons of the telephone at his elbow.

13

Shocks for Inspector Wedge
and Mr. Walker

'Inspector Wedge here,' said the detective as silencing the telephone's jangling, he picked up the receiver.

It was the Inspector at the Commercial Road police station who was speaking. His message was brief and to the point.

'Lang's escaped!' he said.

'Give me the facts . . . and make them quick,' Wedge snapped

As briefly as possible the other told him.

After his arrest in Mr. Walker's junk shed, Lang had been conveyed to the Commercial Road police station to be detained there pending his trial. Of all this Inspector Wedge was of course aware. He, together with Sergeant Matthews and Mr. Walker, had accompanied Lang to the local police station before going on to

Scotland Yard in the early hours of the morning.

Prompted impatiently by Wedge, the officer at the other end of the wire went on to tell him of what had since transpired. It appeared Lang had maintained a morose silence in his cell for the remainder of the night and during the forenoon.

After his lunch had been taken in, and which he had refused to eat, Lang had called for a glass of water. The constable took it in to him and was suddenly attacked and knocked unconscious by a blow on the jaw. Lang had quickly dressed himself in the other's clothes, and slipping through a side door — thus avoiding the desk sergeant and other constable on duty — into the police station yard, mounted a bicycle and rode away.

It was a daring and well-conceived escape, typical of the man who had made it. And it looked as if Lang stood a good chance of remaining at liberty for some time. If also he could find a method of getting out of the country, which he might quite possibly do, there was every chance that he could avoid paying the penalty for his crimes.

Inspector Wedge rapped out some instructions to the man on the other end of the 'phone and hung up his receiver. He picked up an internal telephone, pressed a bell and within a few moments the machinery of Scotland Yard was set in motion for the apprehension of the wanted man.

★ ★ ★

It was early evening when Mr. Walker — unaware of the events that had occurred at the police station not far distant — reached his house in the little cul-de-sac off the Commercial Road. He trundled his barrow round to the side-entrance, unlocked the shed where he kept his curious stock-in-trade and which had but a few hours before been the scene of Lang's dramatic arrest, and put the barrow away for the night. Then he rescued the aspidistra and took it into the house with him.

As he had thought, it made a very welcome addition to the bamboo stand. When he had watered it, and wiped the leaves with a damp cloth, it looked quite a handsome, if somewhat dejected, plant.

He had his supper, followed it with a pipe of his favourite tobacco, and, feeling pleasantly tired after a hard day's work, retired early to bed.

It was with an unexplained sound ringing in his ears that he suddenly woke. It had been a loud sound from somewhere quite near, sufficient to penetrate to his sleeping brain, and wake him, without impressing anything more tangible on his senses than that it was a noise. He sat up in bed and listened. Everything was quite silent again. Most likely what he had heard was only the exhaust of a car in the Commercial Road. And then there came suddenly to his straining ears the sound of a movement from below. There was somebody in the house! Quite distinctly he could hear the creak of stealthy feet moving along the passage. The boards had always been loose.

He slipped out of bed, thrust his feet into his carpet slippers, grabbed a box of matches from the table beside his bed, and tiptoed to the door. Opening it, he made his way to the head of the stairs, and listened again. This time he could plainly hear somebody fumbling at the fastenings of the front door and called loudly:

' 'Oo's that? Wotcher doin'?'

There was a gasp and a crash. Something that sounded like china breaking. Then a cold wind swept up the stairs, followed by the unmistakable slamming of the door and the noise of rapidly retreating footsteps.

The footsteps, Mr. Walker decided, of a man.

He lumbered downstairs, and struck a match. The first thing he saw, lying just inside the closed door, was the remains of the bowl that had housed the aspidistra. It was broken into a dozen pieces. The second thing was the aspidistra itself still in its earthenware pot, forlornly occupying the centre of the strip of carpet that ran down the middle of the narrow passage.

Mr. Walker stood and stared at it in bewilderment, rubbing his dishevelled head. Evidently somebody had tried to pinch his aspidistra. They had been in the act of making off with it when he had disturbed them.

Suddenly the hair on his head prickled, for from behind him came the sound of a smothered groan. He turned sharply, and gave a grunt of pain as the match burned his fingers and went out. As quickly as he could he struck another. The groan had come from beyond the partly open door of the sitting room. Approaching it warily, Mr. Walker pushed it wide and peered in.

Something dark lay sprawling by the window, and he caught his breath. With fumbling hands he lit the gas, and in the cold, incandescent light, saw that the 'something' was the figure of a man, and where he lay the carpet was stained a deeper crimson.

Stooping, he looked down at the pale face, and the glazed, staring eyes. The man was dead, and there was no need to wonder now what the sound was that had woken him. He had been shot. A hole had been neatly drilled through his forehead by a bullet. A revolver lay on the floor by his side.

Mr. Walker, shivering in his capacious nightshirt, stared down at the dead man with wide eyes and dropped jaw. This was murder! And the murderer had got away and left his victim to die on the floor of the little sitting room.

The first shock of his unexpected discovery was passing. Curiosity was taking its place. What had brought these two men to his little house that night? Surely they hadn't gone to all that trouble to try to pinch an aspidistra? And how had they known it was there?

No doubt about it, it was a bit of a teaser. Who was the dead man, and why had his pal shot him? Question after question tumbled over each other in Mr. Walker's brain, but he found no corresponding answers. Gingerly he bent down and examined the man on the floor. He was a small man with rather long, and oily black hair. His face was pitted with smallpox. He was dressed, beneath the light raincoat, in a tight-fitting, rather overtailored brown suit. His shirt was silk, and his narrow, black shoes patent leather. Mr. Walker had seen many of his type round the vicinity of Soho.

He searched the pockets of the dead man, but there was nothing to identify him. It seemed as though he had taken the precaution of removing anything of the sort before setting out to pay his midnight visit.

'Wot did 'e come 'ere arter?' breathed Mr. Walker, squatting heavily back. 'An' wot did the other bloke come for, an' wot 'appened? Luv us! It's a proper teaser!'

He picked up the revolver. It was fully loaded. He could see the shining ends of the cartridges in the cylinder.

'Wot do I do, now?' he said below his breath, as he put the weapon back where he had found it. 'S'pose I oughter get 'old of a copper, an' tell 'im wot's 'appened. Better go an' put some clobber on first, though. Or I'll be catchin' me death o' perishin' cold!'

As he went out into the passage with the intention of going up to his bedroom his eyes lighted once more on the aspidistra. That was the queer thing. Why had the other man tried to get away with that? The plant was almost worthless.

He stooped and picked it up. The china bowl was smashed to pieces, but the flowerpot was still intact, though the earth in it was loosened. In the light that streamed through from the open door of the sitting room, he examined the aspidistra carefully. It appeared to be a very ordinary plant, a good specimen of its kind, but with nothing about it to warrant anyone breaking into a man's house. Perhaps there was something hidden in the earth round the roots. With a fat forefinger Mr. Walker prodded the mould. Then it suddenly occurred to him it might be better if he waited until the police had seen it.

'I'll only be gettin' meself inter trouble if I goes messin' about,' he thought. 'An' there's goin' ter be trouble enough, by the looks o' things.'

Little did he guess how near the mark his conjecture was to prove. And how tightly he himself was to be caught up in a mesh of mystery and drama.

He stood the plant on the lower step of the stairs and went up to dress himself.

When he came out into the street there was no sign of a policeman anywhere, and he looked about him disgustedly.

'Never can find a copper when yer wants one,' he grunted. 'When yer don't they're as thick as flies!'

It was a pity it wasn't daytime, he reflected. Then he would have been able to telephone Inspector Wedge at Scotland Yard. This was just the job for him, he decided grimly. The thought of telephoning the local police station was a good one, he felt, however, and he made up his mind to act upon it.

There was a public telephone box towards the Commercial Road end of the street, and Mr. Walker ambled over to it. He was quickly connected with the police station, and explained what had happened to the desk-sergeant.

'All right,' said the gruff voice, after it had rapidly fired several questions, 'you go back and wait. We'll be sending along as soon as possible.'

'Well, that's that!' thought Mr. Walker,

as he left the callbox and retraced his steps. 'I can't do no more fer the moment. It's up to the coppers now.'

He reached his house, and was searching for his key, when, to his utter and complete astonishment, the front door was suddenly jerked open and a girl confronted him.

14

Mr. Walker gets into trouble

'Oh!' the girl gasped, and in her agitation nearly dropped the object she carried tucked under her left arm. With bulging eyes, Mr. Walker saw it was the aspidistra. He grabbed at the plant, and pulled it away from her.

'Now, look 'ere — ' he began, but she didn't wait to look anywhere. With a sudden movement she ducked past him and, tearing down the little path, was gone.

He made a half-hearted attempt to follow her, realised that his bulk would render such a procedure useless, and came back to his house scratching his head.

He went inside, shut the door, and peered into the lighted sitting room. The dead man still lay sprawling by the window, as he had left him, and Mr.

Walker heaved a sigh of relief. He would have been quite prepared to find the dead body had vanished. Such extraordinary things seemed to have happened to him lately, either in his junk-shed or in his house, he would have been prepared for anything. Still, he told himself, it would have been awkward if the police arrived expecting to find a body, and he hadn't one to show them!

He set the aspidistra down once more on the lower stair. There must be something peculiar about that ancient plant. It seemed to attract people like a honeypot attracted wasps. The girl had been after it, too. She must have been hiding in the house all the time. Or perhaps she had slipped in by the back while he had gone to notify the police.

He was curious to find how these people had got in, and went to find out. It didn't take him long. The kitchen window was open and there were marks on the catch, showing where a knife had been slipped between the sashes.

It seemed ridiculous that anybody should break into his small home, but certainly somebody had. And not only broken in but shot a man.

He was still puzzling over the problem when the police arrived.

Inspector Elliot, of G Division, had plenty on his mind. It was he who had been on the telephone earlier to Inspector Wedge, to report the escape of Lang. And now there was this business of a dead man being found by some Mr. Walker or someone that had suddenly cropped up.

Inspector Elliot sighed. He didn't look like getting a decent night's sleep for a week or two what with one thing and another.

With him were a sergeant and two constables.

When they all crowded into Mr. Walker's little sitting room they seemed to fill the entire place. There was certainly no room for Mr. Walker himself, and he took refuge in the open doorway, and from that point of vantage watched the subsequent proceedings.

A very careful examination was made of the room and the dead man by Elliot and the sergeant. His fingerprints were taken and the revolver was tested for prints. A thorough search was made of his clothing, and Elliot commented on the emptiness of his pockets.

'I could 'ave saved yer that trouble, chum,' volunteered Mr. Walker. 'I 'ad a peep meself, an' there wasn't nothink — '

'You shouldn't have touched anything,' said Elliot severely. 'Did you touch the weapon at all?'

Mr. Walker admitted he had picked it up to look at, and Elliot clicked his teeth.

'We'd better have your prints, too,' he said. 'Take his dabs, will you, Pearson?'

The sergeant came forward with his apparatus, and Mr. Walker's fingertips were pressed upon the inked pad, and from thence to a sheet of glazed card. Just as this had been done the doctor arrived. He made a quick examination and pronounced that death had been the result of a bullet penetrating the brain.

'Death would have been instantaneous,' he remarked at the conclusion of his inspection.

'That coincides with your story,' said Elliot, looking across at Mr. Walker. 'Now tell us exactly what happened, will you?'

Mr. Walker complied, and was listened to in silence.

'Humph!' grunted Elliot, when he had finished. 'It's a queer story. What did these two want to break in for?'

'That's wot I wants ter know, chum. Seein' as 'ow that there aspidistra was in the 'all where the other bloke dropped it, I should say they was after that.'

'That doesn't seem likely to me.' And Elliot rubbed at his moustache. 'Why should anyone want to commit a burglary for a plant that you could pick up anywhere for next to nothing?'

'Ask me another, chum.'

'And what about this woman? You say she had the plant in her arms when she came out of the door?'

'S'right.'

'What was she like? Would you recognise her again?'

The junkman shook his head. 'Dark it was, an' I only see 'er fer a jiffy, chum,' he explained. 'Just 'ad time ter snatch the thing from 'er arm, I did, and then she 'opped it. It wasn't no use me tryin 'ter catch 'er. She could run four times as fast as wot I could.'

'I suppose it wasn't her who ran away in the first place?' suggested Elliot.

'No, it wasn't. It was a man the first time, sure as eggs! Yer could tell by the sound of his footsteps.'

The other frowned.

'Three of 'em,' he muttered. 'It's a mighty queer business. Three people after an aspidistra and one of 'em gets shot — '

'Excuse me, sir,' the sergeant interrupted him. 'The only prints on this pistol belong to this man.' He jerked his head towards Mr. Walker.

'Eh? Oh, they do, do they?' Elliot shot a quick glance at Mr. Walker.

'Well,' said that individual, 'didn't I tell yer as 'ow I picked the thing up?'

The divisional-inspector grunted, and turned to the sergeant.

'All right, Pearson. See if you can find any other prints anywhere else.'

'If you won't want me any more,' put in the doctor, 'I'll be getting along. I've been up every night this week, so far, and — '

'No, that's all right, doctor, you get

along,' Elliot interrupted the other's grievance. 'Drop your report into the station on your way, will you? Thanks. Good night.'

'Goodnight.'

'Now,' said Elliot, when the doctor had gone, 'show me the way these people are supposed to have got in.'

'I'll show yer the way they *did* get in, chum,' retorted Mr. Walker. 'There ain't no 's'pose' about it!'

He led the way to the small kitchen and pointed out the open window and the scratches on the hasp.

The superintendent examined them, peered at the windowsill, and craned his neck out, turning his head from left to right.

'What's below here?' he inquired.

'Concrete,' answered Mr. Walker succinctly.

'So that there would be no traces, eh?' The other withdrew his head. 'That's a pity. Um . . . Well, let's have a look at that aspidistra.'

Mr. Walker took him to the foot of the staircase and showed him the plant standing in its pot on the bottom stair. Elliot picked it up and looked at it.

'No use testing this for prints. They wouldn't show on this earthenware.'

He carried the aspidistra into the kitchen, and after a careful inspection of it, loosened the earth around the roots by tapping the pot gently on the edge of the table and lifted the plant out. It came away from the pot easily and he shook the earth free of the roots, watching closely, with Mr. Walker leaning over his shoulder. But there was nothing but earth. Presently, it lay in a little heap on the table and the roots of the aspidistra, like a queer kind of fish, showed nakedly.

'There's nothing here. Just an ordinary plant. Nobody in their sober senses would commit murder and robbery for that.'

The junkman screwed up his large, florid face in bewilderment. 'But they must 'ave bin arter it, or that feller wouldn't 'ave dropped it in the 'all, an' that girl wouldn't 'ave tried ter get away with it, would she?'

Elliot eyed him levelly. 'Was there any

man, and was there any girl?' he said at last.

'Ain't I already told yer — '

'I know what you've told me,' broke in Elliot meaningly. 'But have you told me the truth? Wait a minute,' he added hastily, as Mr. Walker opened his mouth. 'You've got to admit that this yarn of yours wants a bit of swallowing — '

'It 'appened exactly like I said. Lumme! Look at them scratches on that winder — '

'You could have made them yourself. I'm not saying you did, but you could've done. Look here, Walker, you're well known in this district and everybody speaks very well of you. But this story of yours won't wash, you know. There's no sense in it. Nobody would come after a thing like that plant. Now, why don't you tell me the truth? What happened tonight really? Did you surprise this fellow in the house and shoot him, or what?'

Mr. Walker gaped at him. That his story of what had happened should not be believed had never crossed his mind for a moment.

'Wot I've told yer's the blinkin' truth,'

he asserted indignantly. 'And if yer tryin' ter tell me I'm lyin' — '

'I'm telling you unless you come across with what really happened, I shall have to detain you for further inquiries,' was the snapped reply. 'I don't believe a word of this nonsensical story you've put up.'

Mr. Walker argued and expostulated, but it was no good. Inspector Elliot was sympathetic, but firm, and when he returned to the police station in Commercial Road Mr. Walker went with him, if not with 'the bracelets on,' at least 'detained pending further inquiries'.

Which after all is but a polite way of saying that a man is under arrest.

15

'A bit of a teaser'

The grey-haired desk-sergeant looked up as Inspector Wedge entered the charge-room of the Commercial Road police station.

'Good evenin', sir,' he said, laying down the pen with which he had been laboriously making entries in the 'Occurrence Book'.

'Evening. Inspector Elliot in?'

'No, sir,' the desk-sergeant answered. 'We had a call 'bout an hour ago. Some chap found shot in a house off Commercial Road. The Inspector's gone along — '

'Any news of Lang?'

'Not a sign.'

'Umph . . . How long will — '

Inspector Wedge broke off in his inquiry as to how long Elliot would be and turned towards the door. He had heard the sound of footsteps that he guessed might prove the answer to that very question.

Inspector Elliot was among the little group of men who came in, but Wedge hardly saw him. Instead he stared in astonishment at another man with him.

'Good heavens!' he murmured. 'Walker!'

The junkman's face lit up as he caught sight of his friend. 'Wotcher, chum!' he greeted. Then with a fruity chuckle, he added: 'Just dropped in ter say ''Ow are yer'?'

'Hallo!' Elliot greeted the man from Scotland Yard, then added, a puzzled frown on his face: 'Do you know Walker?'

'Very well indeed. He's been a great help to me on the Lang Case.'

'Really? But I — I didn't know — '

'Anyway, now yours truly 'as gorn and bin pinched 'isself,' broke in Mr. Walker. 'All through bumpin' up against a murder wot I don't know nothink about.'

'You are only being detained pending further inquiries,' corrected Elliot.

'It seems the same thing ter me, chum,' remarked the junkman. 'You 'as ter go ter clink jest the same.'

140

'There must be some mistake,' said Wedge, frowning.

'I hope there is,' replied Elliot heartily. 'I don't like having to detain him, but it's my duty, and there you are.'

'What's it all about? I'm sure you're making a big mistake.'

'Well, I'll be the first to be pleased if I am,' declared the other sincerely. As briefly as possible Elliot explained what had transpired at the little house off the Commercial Road during the night.

Wedge listened attentively, interpolating a question now and again during the recital. When it was finished, he pursed his lips.

'It's a very strange business,' he commented, 'But I think you're making a mistake in believing that Walker had anything to do with the death of this man. I'm willing to vouch for the fact that his story, incredible though it sounds, is true.'

'Thank yer, chum.'

'Well, I hope you're right,' said Elliot, but he sounded a little dubious.

'I'm sure I'm right. You say there was

nothing about this aspidistra that was at all strange?'

'Nothing! I went over it with a fine tooth comb, and it was an ordinary plant.'

'And yet these people were apparently so very anxious to get hold of it,' murmured Wedge thoughtfully. 'How did it come into your possession, Walker?'

Mr. Walker recounted the story of his bargain with Miss Tillington.

'Why was she selling them?' asked Wedge, when he had finished.

'Couldn't tell yer, chum. She just wanted ter get rid of 'em, I s'pose.'

Wedge frowned, and blew a cloud of smoke from the cigarette in his holder.

'Look here,' he said suddenly, turning to Inspector Elliot, 'I think I'll butt in on this and make one or two inquiries.'

Elliot gave him a glance, his eyebrows slightly raised, which Wedge interpreted and answered quickly:

'Oh, I know I've got this Lang business to handle,' he said, 'but at the same time I mustn't leave Mr. Walker here in the lurch.'

The subject of this remark gave a

throaty chuckle, and the Scotland Yard detective flashed him a quick smile. Elliot nodded and the other went on.

'Besides,' he murmured, 'there's not much more I can do about our friend Lang until we get some fresh news on him — which, incidentally, is what I came down to see you about.'

There followed a short discussion between the two detectives, during which Elliot was unable to add any further information as to the escaped man's present whereabouts other than what Wedge already knew. The neighbouring vicinity was being combed for him without so far any success. It seemed pretty evident Lang was not using any place in the surrounding district as a hideout. It looked as though the bird had flown further afield.

Mr. Walker's reaction to this discussion was one of great astonishment. Mouth agape and eyes popping, he listened to the two detectives and drank in from their words the facts about Lang's sensational bid for freedom.

Satisfied his colleague had taken, and

was taking all possible steps towards capturing the criminal, Wedge now turned his attention to Mr. Walker's problem. It seemed to him if the junkman's story of what had taken place at his house that night was true — and Wedge had no doubt about this — there must be something very remarkable connected with the aspidistra. That being so, it appeared obvious to him that the first thing to do in order to clear Mr. Walker of the suspicion against him was to interview Miss Tillington. She should know something about the history of this very unordinary plant.

Another point occurred to him that he made to Elliot.

'Have you yet been able to discover the identity of the dead man?' he asked. 'That should show some light on the affair.'

'I've got his prints. Perhaps your people up at the Yard will be able to tell us who he is.'

Inspector Wedge nodded and fitted a fresh cigarette into his holder. As he lit it he murmured: 'You'd better take great care of that aspidistra and the flowerpot.

Did you examine the pieces of the broken bowl, by the way?'

'Yes, but there was nothing. It was just an ordinary bowl, quite a cheap one.'

'Bit of a teaser, ain't it, mate?' put in Mr. Walker. 'Lumme, some queer things do 'appen to me, don't they!'

'They do,' said Wedge with a little smile, 'and I'd say this was about the queerest so far — '

'Touchwood!' added Mr. Walker, looking hard at Elliot's head as if undecided whether he should touch that or not. Inspector Wedge alone of the others caught the significance of his glance and his saturnine features relaxed in a broad grin. While Mr. Walker flashed him a mischievous wink.

The Scotland Yard detective turned to Elliot. 'If I make myself responsible for Walker will that be all right with you?'

'Well, it's a bit irregular of course, but — '

'You haven't made any official charge yet, and the only reason you want to detain him really is because you're not satisfied with his story. All the same,

145

though, he needn't necessarily be kept here. I'll take charge of him and I can assure you he won't try and make a bolt for it.'

'S'right, chum,' nodded Mr. Walker vigorously.

'Of course,' said Elliot to Wedge, 'if you're prepared to take the responsibility that's all right.'

'Fine,' returned the Scotland Yard man, and addressing Mr. Walker, he went on: 'I think we'll make a start by taking a look at the aspidistra. Perhaps you'll take me along to your house, eh?'

'Why yes, chum — anythink ter oblige, that's me all over.'

Wedge turned again to Elliot.

'I take it that's where the aspidistra is?' he queried.

'Oh, yes, and you'll find a constable on duty there.'

A few minutes later Mr. Walker and Inspector Wedge were on their way in a police car, to the junkman's house, and that rotund individual was remarking to his long and lean companion:

'Bit o' luck fer me, chum, wasn't it, you

'appening ter pop in like yer did?'

'Yes,' smiled Wedge. 'You know, it looks as if you've bumped into something again. I have a queer feeling that in some way there's a connection between the man found murdered in your house and Lang.'

Mr. Walker gaped at him. 'Yer don't mean yer think 'e done it?' he said hoarsely.

Inspector Wedge said: 'Just an idea . . . there may be nothing in it. At first glance, it looks to me as if two separate lots of people broke into your place tonight. The man who was killed, and the man who shot him.'

'And the girl,' put in the junkman. The other nodded.

'And the girl,' he agreed. 'Now which side was she on? Was she working with the murdered man, or was she with his murderer? I'm inclined to think she was with the murdered man.'

' 'Ow d'yer make that out, chum?' asked Mr. Walker.

'It seems to me,' answered the detective, as the sergeant at the wheel turned the car into Commercial Road, 'as if she'd been waiting for the dead man. When he didn't come, she went to find him. If she'd been with the other she'd've gone off with him.'

'Unless she stopped be'ind to get 'old o' that there aspidistra,' offered Mr. Walker shrewdly.

'I don't think that's likely. If she'd been with the murderer, she would have known he'd shot the other man. That being so, I don't think she'd have ventured into the house, however great the provocation.'

'It seems a bit queer there was two lots of 'em arter the same thing, don't it?' muttered the junkman.

'The whole thing's queer. People don't as a rule commit burglary and murder for the sake of a plant, except perhaps in the case of some species of rare orchid, or something of that kind. The thing puzzling me is what value can it have?'

'That's wot's puzzlin' me, too, chum . . . Ah, well, 'ere we are at the old ancestral 'ome.' The car came to a stop at the gate of Mr. Walker's small abode, and the junkman and the detective got out.

The constable on duty answered their knock, and they entered.

The aspidistra lay on the kitchen table as Elliot had left it after his inspection. While Mr. Walker went upstairs to collect one or two things, for the inspector was putting him up for the night at his own home, Wedge examined it carefully. He had hoped to find something that Elliot had overlooked, but he was disappointed. It was just an ordinary aspidistra, apparently no different in any way from the hundreds of others that graced the various sitting rooms of the people who were fond of that kind of decoration.

Mr. Walker joined him, with a dilapidated bag, as he was carefully putting the plant back in its pot.

'Find anything, chum?'

'Nothing.'

'Looks like it could do with a drop o' water,' said Mr. Walker, eyeing the wilting aspidistra a little gloomily. 'I'll just give it a drop afore we go.'

'I'll take a look at the sitting room,' said the detective.

The body had been removed, but

otherwise the little room was exactly as it had been when Mr. Walker made his gruesome discovery. The detective made a careful examination, but found nothing. Neither did the hall yield any results.

'I think that's all we can do here,' he remarked, when he had finished. 'And all we can do tonight. Tomorrow we'll pay a visit to this Tillington woman, and see what she can tell us about this plant which seems to be so popular with somebody.'

16

Miss Tillington explains

Early the following morning Inspector Wedge and Mr. Walker, with a sergeant, unobtrusively in the background, stood on the step of Miss Tillington's house in Bloomsbury.

The front door was opened by a tired-eyed and rather red-nosed maid. She demanded to know what they wanted in an adenoidal voice that accounted for the redness of her nose.

'I'll call the mistress,' she said thickly, sniffing violently. 'Will yer waid, please?'

They waited, and presently Miss Tillington appeared. She eyed them with some distrust.

'What is the reason for this visit?' she demanded, and then, suddenly recognising Mr. Walker: 'Aren't you the man to whom I sold those things yesterday?'

'S'right, mum.'

'It is about them we've called,' murmured Inspector Wedge pleasantly. 'I should like to ask — '

'If this man has been getting into any trouble,' interrupted Miss Tillington, jumping to a totally erroneous conclusion, 'it is nothing whatever to do with me. I sold him several articles I wanted to get rid of, and — '

'That is what I wanted to see you about. Had these things been in your possession for long?'

'Really, I cannot understand what that has to do with you.'

'Perhaps you will understand better when I tell you a serious crime has been committed. And it's the opinion of the police that one of these articles you sold to Mr. Walker forms an important clue.'

Miss Tillington's demeanour underwent a change.

'A serious crime?' she repeated feebly. 'I — I don't — that is — '

'It's rather public here,' broke in the inspector. 'Is there anywhere we could have a word with you in private?'

Miss Tillington led the way into a very

ornate and very modern room that struck Inspector Wedge as being one of the most uncomfortable places he had ever seen. It had also a rather depressing effect on Mr. Walker.

'Now,' she said, when she had closed the door. 'Will you kindly explain yourself, please?'

The detective did so bluntly, assisted occasionally with a word from the junkman. Miss Tillington listened, her thin face showing the dismay his words produced. 'So, you see,' he concluded, 'what I'm anxious to discover is what makes this aspidistra so valuable to these people. There must be something unusual about it that we have failed to find. That something, whatever it is, must have been accomplished by somebody who had access to the plant at some time.'

'All the things I sold to this man were a legacy from my uncle,' said Miss Tillington. 'They were only in the house a few hours.'

'A legacy from your uncle?' repeated Wedge quickly, and Walker saw his eyes narrow. 'I should like to hear the details, if you don't mind, Miss Tillington.'

'I'm afraid there are not many,' she answered reluctantly. 'My uncle died some three weeks ago. As I was the only relative of his living, the solicitors informed me that his property would come to me. It was not worth very much. Just a few old sticks of furniture, and — '

'That there aspidistra!' put in Mr. Walker.

Miss Tillington gave him a freezing stare.

'I take it,' said Inspector Wedge, 'your uncle died without making a will, since you, as the next of kin, inherited his estate?'

'No will was found,' said Miss Tillington. 'I must say I was surprised that my uncle should have apparently died in such poverty. I was always under the impression he was a rich man.'

'That's interesting. Where did your uncle live?'

'In a small cottage in the middle of Dartmoor.'

Miss Tillington's tone of voice suggested that this was almost a criminal proceeding. 'He had lived there for years. He was rather eccentric in his habits — '

'And these odds and ends of furniture, and the aspidistra, were all you received? There was no money?'

'There was not,' said Miss Tillington, her thin lips compressing tightly.

'But your uncle must have had money,' pursued the detective. 'How did he live?'

'I have no idea,' Miss Tillington answered. 'I had not seen him for years. If, however, there had been any money I should have been notified of the fact by his solicitors.'

'Who are they, by the way?'

'Moule and Castle. Their offices are in Tavistock.'

The detective noted down the name in his pocketbook. 'And your uncle's name?' he asked.

'Pringle. Elias Pringle.'

'Thank you,' murmured Wedge, adding the name to that of the solicitors. 'Now just one more question, Miss Tillington. What did your uncle die from?'

'I believe he had a stroke,' she answered after a pause. 'But I'm really not sure what it was. He lived entirely alone. He had been dead a week when he was found.'

'And you were always under the impression he was a rich man? Had you any particular reason for thinking so?'

'No.' Miss Tillington shook her head. 'But I always did think so. I suppose it was because he never did anything, any work of any sort, I mean.'

'That wouldn't necessarily mean he was rich,' said Wedge. 'He might have had just enough to live on, without any margin. Perhaps that was why he chose such an out of the way spot. Living would be cheap there.'

'I suppose so. Very probably that was it. I was always brought up to believe Uncle Elias was very well off.'

That was all, apparently, that could be got from Miss Tillington. It was not much, but it gave the man from Scotland Yard something to work on.

Mr. Walker was frankly disappointed.

'Well, chum,' he remarked, as they left Miss Tillington's neat abode. 'There wasn't much ter be got there, was there?'

'Not a lot. But we've learned something. Whatever there is that happened to that aspidistra of yours which seems to make it different from all other aspidistras must have happened while it was in the possession of Pringle. That looks pretty obvious.'

Mr. Walker agreed.

'I s'pose,' he said reflectively, 'it couldn't 'ave nothink to do with a will. When the old girl said 'e'd died without leavin' a will, it struck yours trooly as 'ow — '

'It occurred to me, too,' interrupted the detective. 'But there's nothing hidden in the plant, or in the pot. It might have something to do with there being no money, though. Miss Tillington may have been right when she thought her uncle was a rich man. He was eccentric, and he may have hidden his money.'

'An' the aspidistra tells yer where, eh, chum?' finished Mr. Walker. 'Lumme! I wouldn't be surprised if yer ain't right. That's why these 'ere people was arter it. But — ' He scratched his head in perplexity. ''Ow do that there plant show where this money's 'id?'

'You're going a bit too fast, Walker,' Wedge smiled. 'We don't know yet if there is any money. It's only conjecture.'

'Well,' said Mr. Walker, 'there must be somethink o' the sort.'

'I'm going to have another look at that aspidistra when we get back. Perhaps a more thorough examination than I've given it up to now will make it yield its secret.'

17

The mystery girl again

When Inspector Wedge, together with Mr. Walker, returned to his office at Scotland Yard he found an urgent message asking him to telephone Inspector Elliot.

Wedge put through the call to the Commercial Road police station immediately. Elliot had two items of news for him. The first being of a startling nature, while the second was the result of routine enquiries.

'The aspidistra's gone!' was the first thing Elliot had to say. It appeared that an hour or so previously a young woman had called at Mr. Walker's house and told the constable on duty that the junkman had sent her to collect some extra articles of clothing, as he was staying elsewhere for a number of days.

So plausible was her story that the officer admitted her into the house and

159

allowed her to go upstairs. It was not until about a quarter of an hour after she had quitted the house, taking with her a bulging suitcase, that he realised the aspidistra had disappeared. By now, of course, there was no signs of the girl.

It seemed fairly apparent that she might be the same girl whom Mr. Walker had encountered.

Elliot's other information was to the effect that the murdered man had been identified as Tonio Ruccio.

'An old member of the Terroni gang,' observed Inspector Wedge. 'Humph, interesting . . . I thought that bunch were all in prison or dead.'

Elliot, from the other end of the wire, went on to say there was still no signs of Lang being picked up. It seemed pretty clear he had made a clean getaway so far as greater London was concerned.

'I suppose there's no evidence that he murdered Ruccio?' asked Wedge.

The other's answer was in the negative, though he agreed it was possible.

'Well, anyway,' the Scotland Yard man said, 'I think the big end of this case and the Lang business lies somewhere well out of London . . .'

There were a few more brief words between them and then Wedge hung up.

'Lumme!' observed Mr. Walker when he was told about the aspidistra and the girl, 'she must 'ave been a pretty cool 'and.'

'It didn't really require that much nerve. She must've been watching your house when you and I arrived there yesterday and seen us leave without the plant. I'm sorry she got away with it.'

He drew his beetling brows together in a frown. 'That aspidistra was our only clue.'

'Did the copper say wot the girl was like?'

'Apparently he described her as a pretty little thing,' said Wedge. 'Quite young. She was fair-haired, and was wearing one of those silver-fox furs — that wasn't all,' he added dryly.

'I should 'ope not!' observed Mr. Walker with a chuckle. 'She'd'ave bin blinkin' cold!'

'Quite,' replied the other. 'She also

161

wore a grey costume and I believe a hat. Not much good trying to trace her from that description. Must be a few dozen girls walking about London in grey costumes and fox furs.'

'S'right, chum.'

Wedge went over to his desk and picked up a timetable. While he studied it the junkman said:

'Wot I wants ter know, is wot do we do next?'

Inspector Wedge glanced at his watch and replied: 'Catch the one-thirty-six to Exeter. We'll just do it.'

'You mean I'm comin' too?'

'Of course. Be a nice little trip for you.'

'But wot about me barrer? Arter all I got me business to think of, ain't I.'

The detective smiled. 'You can take a day or two off, can't you?'

For answer Mr. Walker slowly raised his bulk from the chair in which he had been sitting. 'All right, chum,' he said. 'Anythink ter oblige — that's me all over!'

Inspector Wedge did not consider it necessary for a sergeant to accompany them on their journey, and in a few moments he and Mr. Walker found themselves in a taxi bowling towards Waterloo, from which station they were travelling to Exeter, and from whence they would get a connection to Tavistock.

As they sped down Whitehall and turned left, passing Big Ben, and over Westminster Bridge towards the terminus, Wedge gave his companion an account of how Ruccio had been traced by Elliot.

The murdered man was a member of the notorious Terroni gang that had been broken up several years before. Elliot, armed with Ruccio's fingerprints, had got his record from the Yard, and thus established his identity.

'Wot I don't understand,' said Mr. Walker, 'is 'ow this girl could've got 'erself mixed up with a bloke like this 'ere Ruccio. I saw enough ter know she was a real lidy. Her voice was soft and sort of nice — you know. Even though she only said 'oh' you could tell she was kind of posh.'

'Well, she's in this business, undoubtedly. But whether she was mixed up with

Ruccio is another matter. Maybe I'm wrong and it's the other man she was with.'

'Or 'ow about 'er bein' on 'er own, chum? Playin' a lone 'and like?'

'It's possible, which would mean there were three distinct and separate parties after that aspidistra. Ruccio, the unknown man, and the girl.'

'S'right.'

'It's all very mysterious,' sighed the inspector and he clamped his teeth on his long cigarette holder 'Let's hope our visit to Dartmoor will clear up the mystery a bit. And don't forget, there's our friend Lang to be considered. I've a hunch that when we've cleared up this aspidistra affair we shall find ourselves not far from him. Anyway, we shall see.'

18

The Cottage on the Moor

When Inspector Wedge expressed to Mr. Walker his feeling that the mystery of Miss Tillington's aspidistra was directly, or indirectly, bound up with the man who had escaped from the Commercial Road police station, he was some way towards the truth.

After his audacious escape from the police station, Lang had ridden off in the direction of Aldgate, and driving his bicycle along with the force of a man fleeing to life and liberty, he had torn across Tower Bridge and headed for Streatham and on towards Kingston and Staines. On and on he rode, given, it seemed, the strength of ten men in his desperate bid for freedom.

At Staines he had his first real rest, and with the few coins that were in the constable's trouser pockets, was able to buy himself some food. With the remainder of the money he purchased a cap and a second-hand jacket in a side street shop, which enabled him to discard the constable's coat he had been wearing.

It was evening when he pedalled out of the town and headed in the direction of Salisbury. He rode more easily now, though keeping a wary eye about him. He felt fairly confident that his appearance would not now excite any suspicions. It was growing dark, and to the casual observer he might have been any workman returning home from his daily labours.

Apart from putting as much distance as possible between himself and London, Lang had a definite objective in view. He knew but one person from whom he could obtain sufficient money that would give him the means of quitting the country. He was determined to reach that person as soon as possible.

To do this meant a considerable distance yet to be covered, and he realised he must obtain a speedier form of transport.

He was riding through a small village in the gathering night when the means for carrying out the idea he had been toying with presented itself to him. As he passed an inn he saw a car draw up outside. It was an open two-seater. The driver jumped out and dashed into the inn.

Lang reacted instantly. He dismounted, placed the bicycle against a wall and retraced his steps a few yards back to the inn.

He looked inside the open car and to his delight saw that the driver had left the ignition key. Possibly he had just dashed inside the inn to answer an urgent call of nature, or perhaps to make an emergency telephone call . . . Evidently, in the dark the driver had not noticed him.

Lang glanced about him and saw that the village was no more than a collection of a few houses, and the street that he was in was deserted. Provided he could once get away in the car, he stood every chance of putting miles between him and the village before any of the inhabitants could find another vehicle in which to pursue him.

He jumped into the driver's seat of the car, which was pointed in the direction he wanted to go. He released the brake, let in the clutch, and in an instant was shooting down the street.

It was a fairly old machine and it rattled a bit as with his foot jammed hard on the accelerator, he left the village behind. He heard no shouts or alarm from the inn and for all he knew, or cared, no one had noticed his bold theft.

The needle of the speedometer on the dashboard in front of him quivered and remained on the fifty mark and that seemed to be the best he would get out of the machine. Still, he told himself, it was good enough.

Glancing at the petrol gauge, he was delighted to see the tank was full. Luck, so far, was on his side. If he kept away from the main roads the car should carry him as far as he wanted to go.

Congratulating himself, Lang relaxed in his driving seat and without slackening speed, drove on through the night towards Salisbury.

Once on the other side of that town he

felt he could afford to find some quiet lane in which to halt and snatch a few hours sleep before continuing his journey west.

★ ★ ★

Although they were able to catch a connection from Exeter fairly soon after their arrival there, Inspector Wedge and Mr. Walker found by the time they reached Tavistock it was too late to call on Messrs. Moule and Castle.

They sought out a comfortable inn, where Wedge engaged rooms. After a meal, to which they did full justice the detective got into conversation with the landlord over a pint of beer in the bar.

Casually he brought up the subject of the eccentricities of people in general, and then manoeuvred the conversation till they were discussing the particular eccentricities of the late Mr. Elias Pringle.

The landlord had known him, and was not averse to talking about him. It appeared that many people had talked about him, for he had been quite a character in the district.

He had lived in a small stone cottage up on the open moor, but he had often visited Tavistock to buy food and tobacco. He had been a queer, reserved old man, according to the landlord, and most people had thought him a little mad.

The Cottage was shut up and empty, and in the landlord's opinion, it would remain empty for a long time. Mr. Walker listened to the conversation, interpolating a word here and there, with interest. This dead uncle of the rather starchy Miss Tillington must have been a queer old bloke, he thought, to bury himself away in the middle of Dartmoor. Or had he had some object for that? Maybe it was just that he liked to be alone. There were people like that.

It wouldn't have suited him, thought Mr. Walker. He liked company and people.

Wedge had brought the subject of money up. No, the landlord didn't think old Pringle had been well-off. He had had enough to pay his way, but he wasn't a rich man. At least, if he had been he'd kept the fact to himself. In most people's opinion he had been poor.

'How far away is this cottage?' asked the detective, draining his tankard. The landlord became voluble. It was a matter of about three miles, he explained. You took the road out of the town and kept on until you came to a little knot of trees and the cottage was there.

The detective changed the subject. He began to talk about the political situation, listened to the landlord's views on what attitude the Government should adopt, and finally suggested a walk before turning in.

Mr. Walker agreed.

'We may be late,' said Inspector Wedge, 'could I have a key, do you think?'

The obliging landlord not only thought so, but produced a key which, he said, would admit them by the side door.

'Come along, Walker,' said the detective, when they were outside the inn. 'We'll go and inspect this cottage in which the eccentric Mr. Pringle lived and died. I'm rather anxious to have a look.'

'Anythink to oblige, chum,' said Mr. Walker.

It was a clear moonlit night, and they set off towards the open moor, which they could see rolling greyly away in the distance. In a little while they had left the outskirts of the town and struck a moor path, which wound its way over the melancholy expanse. In the light of the moon there was a grandeur about that sombre scenery that made them both silent.

Here was nature, grim and uncompromising. Beside the great crags and massifs, and the wide stretches of scrub, mankind with its petty problems and petty quarrels seemed dwarfed and remote.

Here on that grey expanse, man had crawled about in skins, had made his flint arrows, and hunted his food. Had lived in rough stone huts and died. This moor was unchanged, in a changing world — a mightier and less vulnerable place than the greatest city. An epitaph to the past and a monument to the future.

They came at last to the trees the

landlord had mentioned. They were a small copse of stunted pines, twisted and battered from long exposure to many storms, and in their shadow nestled a small grey cottage. It was built entirely of stone, and surrounded by a low wall that enclosed a patch of neglected garden.

'Looks a pretty lonely spot, don't it, chum?' remarked Mr. Walker.

Wedge said nothing. In the clear, cold white light of the moon the moorland cottage did look lonely, but it possessed a singular beauty of its own. There was not another habitation of any kind within sight. On all sides the moor rolled away to the jagged horizon.

Leaving the narrow path, the detective approached the cottage. There was no gate — only an opening in the wall marked the entrance. With Mr. Walker at his heels, Wedge entered the garden and made his way up a weed-covered path to the stone porch. The weather-beaten door was locked, as he had expected, but by its side was a window, grimed with dirt. With his handkerchief the inspector wiped one of the small panes of glass and peered in.

Inspector Wedge found himself looking into a small room. By the light of the moon he was able to see that, except for what appeared to be a heap of rubbish on the floor, it seemed completely empty. It was a low-ceilinged room, and at one side he was able to make out an open fireplace.

'Wot was the idea of comin' 'ere, mate?' asked Mr. Walker, as Wedge straightened up from his scrutiny.

'Curiosity,' answered the detective, 'and a hope that we might learn something. I'm going to have a look inside,' he continued. 'There should be a window somewhere we could get through. Let's see what there is round at the back.'

He led the way round the side of the cottage, and surveyed the rear of the premises. There was a back door, which on inspection proved to be locked also, and a window that admitted light to a small kitchen.

He examined the catch, and found it was a very simple affair. Taking a penknife from his pocket, he opened the largest blade, and slid it between the sashes. A slight pressure and the catch snapped back. He pushed up the window.

'In you go,' he said. 'There's plenty of room.'

Mr. Walker hoisted his large bulk on to the sill, and scrambled through. A moment later Wedge joined him and closed the window. Taking a torch from his pocket he switched it on and swept the beam back and forth.

They found themselves in a small kitchen. A dresser ran along one wall, an old range occupied a recess, and there was a copper in one corner. For the rest there was nothing but rubbish and dirt.

Mr. Walker eyed his surroundings with disfavour.

'You didn't expect the Ritz, did you?' Wedge commented. 'It's a typical moorland cottage — no better and no worse. Let's explore.'

The cottage consisted of four rooms. The kitchen and the parlour on the ground floor, and two rooms up the narrow flight of rickety stairs.

'Ain't much ter see, is there, chum?' said the junkman, when they had completed their tour of inspection, and were back again in the kitchen.

'No very little,' said the detective absently. 'Listen! Can you hear anything?'

'I *can* 'ear somethink . . . Sounds like a car — '

'It *is* a car,' said Wedge, as the sound grew louder and more recognisable.

He stepped quickly to the door and entered the empty sitting room. The window commanded a view of the rough moorland road that passed the cottage and he peered intently out.

Presently a small coupé came in sight, slowed outside the cottage, and stopped.

'Now I wonder — ' murmured Wedge, breaking off as the slight figure of a woman got out of the car and turned towards the cottage. The moonlight fell full on her face.

'Lumme!' breathed Mr. Walker, huskily clutching at his companion's arm. 'That's 'er, chum! That's the girl wot come out o' me 'ouse with the aspidistra!'

19

Visitors from the night

'She's coming here,' said the detective, as the girl began to walk towards the gap in the wall. 'Come on, Walker. This is where we make ourselves scarce. Up the stairs!'

With silent rapidity he went over to the staircase and mounted it swiftly, Mr. Walker floundering up after him.

In the dead stillness that surrounded the cottage they could hear the girl's light steps. They came up to the front door and stopped.

'She's trying the door,' whispered the inspector. 'Well, she'll be unlucky there.'

There was an interval of silence, and then the faint steps reached them again. They could trace them as she walked round to the back, and then they stopped once more.

'She's going to use the same method of entry as we did,' murmured the detective.

'And she'll find the window ready for her. I left the catch unfastened.'

In a few seconds he received confirmation of his words for there came a gentle squeak as the sash was raised. It was followed a moment later by the sound of hollow footsteps that echoed through the empty cottage.

Peering down the steep stairway, Wedge saw the flash of a torch and caught a glimpse of a distorted shadow thrown across the whitewashed wall below.

He wondered if the visitor would come up the stairs, but it seemed she had no intention of doing anything of the kind.

He could hear her moving about below but she seemed to be confining her area of operations to the sitting room. With a whispered word to Mr. Walker to remain where he was, Wedge cautiously descended the stairway, one tread at a time. He made no noise, and reached the bottom without betraying his presence to the girl. From here he could see into the sitting room. The girl was kneeling with her back towards him by the old fireplace, apparently scraping at the stone flags that formed the hearth.

Inspector Wedge watched with interest. The task on which she was engaged seemed to be taking a long time, and she was not hurrying. Carefully, and without the slightest idea that her actions were being overlooked, she proceeded. Wedge could not see exactly what she was doing. Her body blocked the view, but he guessed from the sound that she was attempting to remove one of the stone flags.

He waited and watched. Was he about to discover the secret of the eccentric Mr. Pringle and the aspidistra? Had the old man been rich after all, and hidden his money under that stone which the girl was working on so diligently? If so, who was the girl, and how had she discovered the secret? From the aspidistra, in some way? That was all right, but how did she know of the existence of the hiding place? And how did Ruccio and his murderer come into it? They had known, too.

The question flashed through the detective's mind as he watched that slight figure kneeling to its task in the dim light of the torch, which lay on the floor.

The scrape of metal on stone seemed to enhance the surrounding silence, and then from the direction of the kitchen came another sound. It was so faint as to be almost inaudible, but it reached Wedge's sensitive ears, and he turned his head sharply towards the darkness of the kitchen doorway. He could see nothing, but the slight shuffling sound had been unmistakable! There was somebody out there, concealed in the darkness!

He drew back, crouching down under the stairs. The girl had apparently heard nothing, for she was still working away without pause.

The darkness of the kitchen doorway seemed to grow darker and more solid, and then a patch of this darkness came away from its surroundings and began to move silently and stealthily along the narrow passage.

Wedge fixed his eyes on this slowly moving blot, and presently it began to take outline and resolved into the dim, crouching shape of a man. He was dressed in something black and there was no face visible. He came nearer to the door of the sitting room, moving as silently as a shadow, and peered in.

The girl still occupied the same position, and seemed to be completely unaware of this fresh arrival. The man in black stood motionless, in a half stooping position that gave him the appearance of having a humped back, and the inspector from his vantage under the stairs watched them both.

A minute dragged slowly by, while the girl continued to scrape noisily at the stone, and the unknown, like a huge cat waiting to pounce, remained poised on the threshold of the room. It was pretty obvious, thought Wedge, that if these two knew each other the man in black would have made his presence known. He was watching as eagerly as the inspector himself. The detective could almost see the other's tensed muscles.

And then quite suddenly, and without any warning of his intention, he acted. His hand, which had been concealed in the pocket of the long coat he was wearing, came out holding a stubby automatic, and straightening up, he stepped boldly into the open doorway.

'Don't move!' he commanded, in a harsh, rasping voice. 'Don't move, or it'll be the worse for you!'

The girl uttered a queer sound of startled fear, and turned her head.

'Fenner!' she breathed.

'Know me, do yer?' said the man in the doorway, and there was a surprised note in his voice. 'Who are yer?'

She made no reply. Her face had gone white, but she faced him steadily.

'Not going to talk, eh?' said the man she had called Fenner. 'Well, it doesn't matter. How did you get here?'

'I came by car.' Her voice was calm and clear. Wedge, remembering Mr. Walker's description of it, decided it had been a good one.

'I didn't mean that!' snapped the man in black. 'I meant how did you know where to look? I know yer came by car. It was seein' it outside told me there was someone in here.'

'You ought to know how I knew where to look. You were after the same thing, but you weren't clever enough to get it.'

'So you got old Pringle's aspidistra, did yer? I thought the police had got it.'

'The police had, but they didn't keep it,' replied the girl. 'Don't you think you'd better put away that gun? You've done enough damage with guns already.'

'Likely, isn't it? And give you a chance to bring out one of yer own? No blinkin' fear!'

'I haven't a gun, but I don't expect you to believe me. Do you mind if I get up? It's very uncomfortable kneeling like this.'

'It didn't seem ter worry you before,' he retorted. 'No! You stay where you are. If you try any tricks, I'll plug you! I'm warning you.'

'As you murdered Ruccio?'

'Yes, as I plugged Ruccio,' snarled the man, 'and as I'd plug 'im again, the dirty little double-crossin' rat!'

'I'm not going to argue with you over your description of the late Mr. Ruccio,' said the girl. 'You're probably in a better position to judge about that than I am. But I do wish you'd let me get up. I'm getting cramp.'

'You just stay where you are, my girl.' The man edged farther into the room. 'I can't place you at all,' he went on. 'Who are yer?'

'If I told you my name it would convey nothing to you.'

'I don't want ter know yer name. What I want ter know is how you came ter be mixed up in this business?'

'For the same reason as you did,' came the calm reply. 'I want the Fullerton emeralds.'

The breath hissed through Inspector Wedge's teeth. Here was part of the mystery explained. Now he knew why the name of Fenner had sounded vaguely familiar when the girl had mentioned it. The Fullerton emeralds had, seven years ago, filled the newspapers with sensational headlines.

Lord Fullerton had amassed undoubtedly the finest collection of emeralds in the world. He had spent a huge fortune in acquiring them, and the collection had been valued at the enormous sum of three-quarters of a million pounds. The loss to the insurance company that had insured them had been colossal, when they had been stolen, and Fullerton had been inconsolable.

There had been no trace of them, although the police had worked diligently. Neither had the thief been discovered. And now, after all these years, they had cropped up again. There was little doubt in Wedge's mind what was lying under that flagstone in the hearth, on which the girl had been working so energetically.

'Oh, you want the Fullerton emeralds, do yer?' said the man softly. 'And you knew they was here, eh? How did yer know that?'

'It's much too long a story to tell you now. Ask me some other time.'

'P'raps there won't be no other time. You can please yerself about tellin' me. You were getting on mighty well when I interrupted yer, so suppose you go on with the job?' He gestured with the muzzle of the automatic towards the hearth.

'Do all the work while you take the reward,' said the girl scornfully. 'No, thank you! You get on with it yourself!'

'You do as you're told!' snarled the other menacingly. 'While I've got this gun, I've got the whip hand, see? You were trying to shift one o' them stones when I was watching yer. Now go on and finish the job.'

Her mouth set obstinately, and Wedge thought she was going to refuse. But apparently she changed her mind, for with a shrug of her slim shoulders she turned once more to her task.

Fenner, his eyes hard above the handkerchief that he had tied round the lower part of his face, stood watching her.

Inspector Wedge thought quickly. Was there any chance of taking the man by surprise? It seemed remote. At the first movement he would shoot.

He remembered Fenner now. An accomplished safe-breaker, who had been sentenced to a term of ten years for breaking into the City branch of the London and Northern Joint Stock Bank. The night watchman had been beaten up, and that was why the sentence had been such a heavy one. But what had Fenner to do with the Fullerton emeralds? Had he been responsible for that, too? It was possible. They would never have caught him for the bank robbery if a 'nose' hadn't given him away, and that had been six months after. There would have been time in the interval for him to have done the other job, and it had happened between the bank robbery and the time he had been arrested. But how had the emeralds got into old Pringle's cottage? Well, there would be time enough to go into all that later. The present problem was to get Fenner before he had a chance of shooting, and it wasn't easy.

The girl was still busy at the stone. Either it was very difficult to move, or she was pretending it was, to gain time.

At last the girl seemed to have succeeded in her task, for she stopped working suddenly, and looked up at the man in black.

'You'll have to give me a hand,' she said. 'I've chipped away all the cement, but I can't lever the stone. It's too heavy.'

He looked at her suspiciously. 'Trying to catch me?' he laughed unpleasantly.

'I'm not falling for any o' those tricks, my girl.'

'Don't be stupid,' she broke in impatiently. 'If you won't help me, go and try yourself. I'll hold the torch.' She picked it up as she spoke.

'Well, you get over in the corner,' he said, 'an' don't start anything or you'll be sorry.'

With a contemptuous twitch of her shoulders she obeyed. Fenner, without taking his eyes off her, moved over to the fireplace. Wedge could see the instrument she had been working with was a large cold chisel, and it was now stuck between the interstices of two flagstones.

'You'll have to throw your weight on it,' explained the girl. 'The stone should come up then.'

Fenner stooped and laid his hand on the chisel and at that second the girl acted. With a lithe spring she reached him, and before he quite realised she had moved, she brought the heavy torch down hard on the hand holding the automatic. Fenner uttered a sharp cry of pain, and the weapon clattered to the floor. He made a dive to recover it, but he was too late. She had already grabbed the pistol and leapt back.

'Now I think it's your turn to do as you're told,' she said crisply. 'Keep still! I'm just as capable of shooting you as you were of shooting me!'

20

The unknown

The whole thing had been done so neatly and swiftly that Inspector Wedge almost exclaimed his admiration aloud. The girl had taken a risky chance and it had come off.

Fenner broke into a flood of bad language, which was promptly checked by his captor.

'You can stop that,' she snapped, 'or I'll shoot you through the leg. It won't do a lot of damage, but it'll hurt like hell!'

Fenner stopped abruptly.

'That's better,' said the girl. 'Now prise up that stone. You won't find it so difficult as I made out, but I had to get you nearer on some excuse, and that was the best I could think of.'

'I s'pose yer think you're smart — '

'I know I'm smart,' she interrupted coolly. 'Our positions at the moment prove it. Don't talk — move!'

'Look here,' said the man, adopting a conciliatory tone. 'Why can't we make a bargain, eh? There's enough stuff there fer both of us, ain't there?'

'Why should I make a bargain when I can have the lot? I'm making no bargains, Fenner. Shift that stone!'

With a muttered imprecation Fenner bent down over the cold chisel. The girl had moved round so that her back was towards the door, and she blocked Fenner's view. Wedge saw his opportunity. Creeping forward noiselessly he slipped into the room, reached over the girl's shoulder and wrenched the pistol from her grasp.

'I'd like to take a hand in this game, if you don't mind,' he said pleasantly.

The girl swung round with a startled cry, and Fenner straightened up.

'Who the devil are you? Where did you come from?' he demanded hoarsely.

'I've been listening for some considerable time,' replied the detective. 'I was here before either of you arrived.'

Fenner uttered an oath. 'Who are you?'

'I'm Inspector Wedge of Scotland Yard,' the detective introduced himself. Then turning to the girl, he asked quietly: 'Do you feel inclined to tell me your name?'

She hesitated. Then: 'My name is Wyn Trevor.'

'Thank you,' said Wedge gravely. 'Now we are all properly introduced. This — er — gentleman is one Arthur Fenner, a notorious safebreaker, who I think I am right in saying has only recently come out of prison. He looks as if he will shortly go back again — until the date appointed for the execution, of course.'

'What d'yer mean — the execution?' demanded Fenner huskily.

'A small matter connected with the death of Tonio Ruccio. You can't shoot people without paying the penalty, you know, Fenner.'

'He tried ter shoot me first, the little swine! If I hadn't seen what he was up to, an' wrenched the pistol away from him, he'd have done it. That isn't murder, that's self-defence — '

'We've only your word for what occurred,' said the detective. 'However,

I'm not going to argue about that at the moment. I've no doubt you will be able to put forward that defence at your trial. In the meanwhile you might continue with what you were doing when I interrupted you.'

'I'll see you in hell first!'

'You'll do as you're told! I'm not asking you favours. I'm giving you an order. Now, jump to it!'

Fenner's small eyes glinted venomously above the handkerchief. But Wedge had the whip hand, and he knew it. With a muttered curse he stooped once more over the flagstone. The girl craned forward in her eagerness to watch, and Wedge moved a step or two nearer. Fenner leaned on the cold chisel and the flagstone moved. One end rose an inch, and the man inserted his fingers under the edge and pulled. It came up like the lid of a box, working on a pivot at one end, and disclosed an oblong cavity beneath. Fenner peered into this and then lifted out a large chamois leather bag, the mouth of which was secured with cord.

'Open it,' directed Inspector Wedge,

and Fenner fumbled with the knot.

'Drop that, and put up your hands!' rasped a voice from the doorway suddenly. Wedge saw the girl's mouth open in shocked surprise, and stiffened. He had his back to the door and could not see the interrupter, but before he could turn the hard staccato voice came again.

'You with the gun, don't move! If you do I'll drill you through the back!'

The detective realised he could do nothing. If the unexpected newcomer meant what he said — and there was something in his tone warned Wedge he did — it would be foolhardy not to obey him. Therefore he remained motionless, and waited for the next development.

It was not long in coming.

'I seem to have arrived just in time,' remarked the voice. 'Take the gentleman's gun away from him, Fenner.'

But Fenner seemed to have been turned to stone. His eyes, which were all that were visible, were staring beyond Wedge with an expression of abject terror.

'You're dead!' he whispered huskily. 'You're dead.'

'Don't be a fool!' snapped the unknown. 'I'm nothing of the sort! I'm very much alive. Do as I tell you.'

'Then who died?' whispered Fenner. 'Who was the man who died?'

'Never mind that now,' was the impatient reply. 'Get that man's gun — '

'If you attempt to come near me,' said Wedge warningly, 'I shall shoot!'

'If you do, it will be the last thing you will do!' retorted the unseen man behind him. 'Don't listen to his bluff, Fenner. Do as I tell you.'

Fenner approached Wedge a little nervously, and the detective, realising there was nothing else for it, shrugged his shoulders and gave him the pistol.

'That's better,' said the unknown, approvingly. 'Now keep him covered.' He advanced farther into the room. 'I never expected to find the place would be so popular,' he said. 'I can understand what you are here for, Fenner, but who are these other people?'

'He's Inspector Wedge of Scotland Yard,' said Fenner, jerking his head towards the inspector. 'I don't know who the girl is, except she says her name's Trevor.'

'H'm, well, we'd better find out. I'm curious to know — '

'Look out!' cried Fenner in alarm. 'There's somebody behind you.'

The unknown man spun round, but he was just a fraction of a second too late. A hand like a leg of mutton closed on his pistol wrist, and although he pressed the trigger, the bullet only brought down a shower of plaster from the ceiling.

'You keep still, chum,' said Mr. Walker. 'Otherwise, yours trooly'll 'ave ter biff yer over the napper with this 'ere brick, see?'

'Good man,' breathed Wedge, and hurled himself on Fenner.

The man fired wildly, and the detective felt the wind of a bullet as it flew past his head. Before he could fire again Wedge had gripped his wrist, and wrenched his arm behind his back. Fenner struggled and cursed, but he was helpless. The inspector shot out a foot, hooked him round the ankles, and brought him to the floor with a crash. At that moment the torch which the girl had been holding went out.

'Put the light on!' panted the detective, kneeling astride the writhing man on the floor. 'Put the light on, Miss Trevor.'

But the girl made no reply, although he could hear her moving about in the darkness. Fenner was renewing his struggles and the detective had all his work cut out to attend to him. The man still retained possession of the automatic, which he was trying desperately to pull free. But Wedge had no intention of giving him the chance of using it if he could help it. Gripping his shoulders, he tried to keep him down, but Fenner was strong, and as slippery as a snake. He twisted this way and that in a frantic endeavour to break away from the detective's hold, and wrench his arm from under him. But Wedge held on grimly. He could hear a scuffling and grunting from near by, and guessed Mr. Walker was having an equally difficult job with the other man.

And then he heard the sound of a car starting up outside. The engine roared, dwindled, and faded away. The girl had gone! His surprise made him momentarily relax his vigilance, and Fenner took immediate advantage of this. With a sudden heave he rolled over, and gained the uppermost position. Wedge felt the cold muzzle of the automatic press against his neck, and Fenner's breath fanned his cheek as he whispered jerkily:

'Keep quiet, now, will you?'

Wedge lay still.

'That's better,' went on Fenner, breathing heavily. 'Keep still, or — '

There was a rustling movement, and then a bright fan of light split the darkness, as the man switched on a torch, and got shakily to his feet.

He turned to Wedge and growled:

'You stay where you are. If you try to move I'll shoot, so you'd better remember that.'

The detective said nothing but turned his head towards the struggling figures of Mr. Walker and the other man. The bulky form of the junkman was heaving and writhing about the floor like a playful whale. His huge hands were gripping and

198

trying to force away the pistol that the other was struggling to turn towards him.

'Stop that!' snarled Fenner. 'Let go his wrists, will you?'

But Mr. Walker took no notice. Red in the face and panting with his efforts, he continued stubbornly to fight.

Without taking his eyes off Wedge, Fenner went over and gave the junkman a vicious kick. His heavy boot caught him in the side and drove all the breath out of his body. It left his open mouth in a sudden whistling gasp, and his arms dropped.

His adversary, released from his grip, staggered to his feet, breathing jerkily.

'Now,' he said, speaking with difficulty, 'we'll deal with these interfering busybodies. Where's the girl?'

'She's gone,' said Fenner. 'Got scared and bolted, so — '

'Scared nothing!' snarled the other, his eyes sweeping round the little room. 'She's bolted with the emeralds!'

21

Trapped

Inspector Wedge smiled grimly. So that was why the girl had gone! She had taken advantage of the struggle quietly to make off with the wash-leather bag.

'By Cripes, so she has!' exclaimed Fenner as he saw the bag had gone.

'You fool!' snapped the other man, angrily. 'Why did you let her?'

'How could I help it? I had all my work cut out with him.'

'Who is this girl?' rasped the unknown, turning to Wedge. 'She came with you.'

'She did nothing of the kind. I've no more idea than you have who she is.'

'We'd better go after her, hadn't we?' suggested Fenner.

'What chance should we have of catching her after the start she's had? Besides, we can't leave these two.'

'But the emeralds — '

'Shut up for a minute and let me think,' grunted the other.

His bushy brows drawn together, the detective watched him curiously. Who was this man who had put in such an unexpected appearance? Fenner knew him obviously, but his arrival had been as much a surprise to him as to any of them. What had he meant when he said 'you're dead'? Was it possible that . . .

'I've got a car outside.' The unknown's harsh voice broke in on his thoughts. 'Go out and look in the luggage carrier. You'll find some rope. Bring it back here and tie these two up.'

Fenner opened his mouth to say something, thought better of it, and, handing the torch to his companion disappeared into the darkness of the narrow passage.

'I don't know how you came into this business,' remarked the unknown to Wedge, when he had gone. 'But you know too much to be allowed to go free. I've heard of you, but I don't know who your fat friend is.'

'I'll tell yer 'oo I am,' said Mr. Walker,

huskily. 'Walker's the name, an' if I got 'alf a chance, I'd push yer perishin' face in.'

'Well, you won't get even a quarter of a chance,' said the other. 'So you're the Mr. Walker of radio fame, are you? I've heard you. You're the fellow who's always wanting to know, eh? Well, my friend, I'm afraid this is the last little bit of curiosity you're going to enjoy. How did you get on to this business of the Fullerton emeralds?'

'I didn't know nothink about no em'ralds until a few minutes ago.'

The unknown's lined face puckered. 'I don't understand this at all,' he muttered. 'Why did you come here? Who was the girl?'

'If you don't understand, you're in the same position as we are,' said Inspector Wedge. 'Or I should, perhaps, say — were — for I'm beginning to understand quite a lot.'

'Are you?' said the man, and his expression was unpleasant. 'Well, your understanding won't do you much good. It's a pity you should have chosen tonight to come here — a great pity from your point of view. I've — Oh, here you are, Fenner. Did you find that rope?'

Fenner held out a coil of thin rope in his hand for answer.

'Good. I've carried that rope for a long while, and this is the first time I've found a use for it. Tie them up, and see that you do it securely.'

The other obeyed. He certainly made a good job of it, for by the time he had finished, neither Wedge nor Mr. Walker were able to move hand or foot.

'Now gag them,' ordered the unknown, tearing strips from the lining of his overcoat. When this had been done, he pocketed his pistol and surveyed his prisoners with satisfaction.

'I think they're pretty harmless now.'

'But you're not going to leave them here, are you?' demanded Fenner. 'That 'busy' knows me, and — '

'His knowledge won't be of any use to him. Go back to the car and fetch me the two spare cans of petrol.'

Fenner looked at him for a moment in a puzzled way, and then he understood.

'You're going to set fire to the place?' he asked hoarsely, and the other nodded.

'It seems to be a good method of solving the difficulty. We can't leave these two here alive, and murder in cold blood never appealed to me. This cottage is old, and with the assistance of a little petrol, should burn like tinder. There will be no traces — '

'Why not let me put a bullet through them?'

'Bullets leave traces. There will be no traces my way. Even if any remains are found, there will be nothing to show it was murder. It will be put down to accident.'

His voice was entirely devoid of emotion.

'I don't like having to do this,' he went on. 'But it's one of those unpleasant things that have got to be done. They brought it on themselves by interfering with what didn't concern them. Come on, let's get it over as soon as possible.'

Fenner went reluctantly away, and Wedge felt his heart grow cold. If this man carried out his threat, and there seemed no likelihood that he would not, nothing could save them. The cottage, as he had said, was old and would burn furiously. It would only be a matter of seconds before they were overcome by the smoke, and then . . . His imagination conjured up the rest, and he gave an involuntary shiver.

Glancing across at the bound figure of Mr. Walker, he caught the junkman's eye. Mr. Walker's gaze was steady, and he almost imagined that he gave an encouraging wink, but this may have been due to the dim light of the torch.

Fenner came back with the two petrol cans, and set them down. He had removed the handkerchief and his face looked pale. It was an unpleasant face. Thin and shifty. The small eyes were set too near the bridge of the broad nose, and the lips were full and sensual, above a receding chin.

The unknown man gave him the torch to hold while he opened the tins of spirit. When he had done this, he picked up one of the cans and proceeded to sprinkle the floor and the walls liberally.

'We'll use the other for the passage,' he

said, setting down the empty tin and picking up the full one. 'I shan't be long now.'

He picked up the other can and went out of the door. Fenner stood in silence while he was away, licking his lips nervously. He was obviously horrified at the other's scheme, but unwilling to interfere. In a little while the other man came back.

'You'd better carry the empty tins back to the car. We don't want to leave any evidence behind if we can help it, and tins don't burn.'

'Do you want me to come back?' muttered Fenner, picking up the cans.

'Not if you're squeamish. Start the engine and wait for me. I'll finish here and join you in a moment.'

The other departed with alacrity, and the tall unknown surveyed his victims with a set face.

'I think everything is ready,' he said evenly. 'I'm sorry for this, but it can't be helped.'

He went over to the door, took a last look round, and switched out the torch.

For an instant there was darkness, and then came the scraping of a match. The little yellow flame flickered dimly, and then, as he flung the match on the floor, a sheet of blinding light leaped upwards. The doorway, and the man who had stood there, became blotted out as the petrol-soaked boards caught fire. His rapidly retreating footsteps were drowned in the roar of the flame, and somewhere a door slammed.

Inspector Wedge and Mr. Walker strained at the ropes that bound them with a desperate effort to loosen them, but it had no effect. The ropes were strong and the knots refused to give a fraction. The fire was raging by the door, and rapidly gaining ground, the white, smoky flames licking hungrily at the walls. In a few seconds at most the entire room would be ablaze. The heat was terrific and the fumes of the burning spirit caught at the captives' throats. Mr. Walker coughed and choked, and the detective felt his senses reeling, and a deadly faintness steal over him. He tried to ward it off, but it grew stronger. This was the end. Nothing could possibly save either of them now. He heard the car drive away and the noise of the engine diminish to silence, and then a great flood of darkness mercifully engulfed his brain, and he seemed to be falling into a pit that had no bottom.

★   ★   ★

The man in the rattling two-seater skirted Princetown and reached the moor by a circuitous route. He was nearly there, he congratulated himself. Soon he would reach not only a brief sanctuary but someone who would provide the cash necessary to his escape from the country and the long arm of the law, which even now, as he knew full well, was reaching out to grasp him.

It was then that he saw the glow against the night sky. Wonderingly he drew nearer. The source of the glow was not visible to him until his car breasted a ridge. He saw about a hundred yards towards his right the small cluster of trees, twisted and gnarled and black in the glare of the blazing cottage.

Lang drew in his breath sharply and brought the car to a jolting halt. A hundred questions flashed through his mind as he sat and stared at the holocaust. The flames were pouring through a great gaping hole in the roof where it had caved in. The place was doomed. Nothing could save it. The lurid light lit up the bleak moorland and a great column of black smoke shot up to the cloudless sky.

Switching off the engine, Lang got out of the car and cautiously approached the blaze. He took advantage of every tree and scrub, for he was not risking the possibility of there being anyone about — other than the person he had come especially to see. It was when he was some fifty yards away that he saw the car. It had been hidden from his view until then by the burning cottage. Even now he was only in time to watch it drive off — he could neither distinguish its occupants nor see how many there were.

He watched it disappear in the direction of Princetown, before he resumed his progress to the cottage. His approach was still cautious, though it seemed pretty clear to him that the place was empty, or if there was anyone inside they would be far beyond human aid.

Now he was as near the blaze as he could comfortably be. He watched it, his face drawn in bitter, savage lines. Whatever the cause of the fire there was one thing that stood out with terrible clarity, which was that the hopes that had brought him on his long and hazardous journey were utterly doomed.

So far as he knew now, Lang's chances of escape — which, as he had planned it in his mind, would have been possible only with the financial help of the cottage's occupant, were crumbling with the blazing mass before him.

With bitter curses against the fates that had after all turned against him, Lang turned away and proceeded back to his car.

22

Crooks quarrel

The car with the unknown man at the
wheel, and Fenner sitting uneasily beside
him, rushed through the night. Turning,
as they left the wide expanse of open
moorland, they could see the red glow in
the sky and were satisfied.

'That wipes out all future trouble,'
muttered the man at the wheel. 'There's
nobody to talk, and we're safe.'

'What about the girl?' grunted Fenner.
'She's still alive, and she's got the
emeralds.'

'Yes . . . I was forgetting her. Who is
she?'

'I don't know. She wasn't with the
others. She was working on her own. It's
my opinion she's a crook.'

'In that case, she won't be much
danger. I'd like to find out who she is,
though, and try to get those stones back.'

'Where are we making for?' asked Fenner, as they sped through the sleeping Princetown, and bore to the left.

'I've got a house in London,' replied the other briefly. 'We shall be safe there. Nobody will connect me with that cottage, and you can lie low for a bit.'

Fenner began a string of questions that had been puzzling him ever since the other had put in his unexpected appearance at the cottage, but the unknown was not in a communicative mood, and cut short his curiosity.

The journey was long and tiring. They had to stop twice for petrol at a filling station, and they reached the outskirts of London heavy-eyed and weary.

The unknown drove to a large and imposing looking house near Regent's Park, where he and his companion ate a meal, and when it had been eaten suggested that they should get some sleep.

Fenner, who was finding it difficult to keep his eyes open, agreed to the suggestion with alacrity, and was shown to a comfortable room, where he quickly slipped into a soft bed and was almost instantly asleep.

It was evening when he woke, and after a wash went downstairs to seek his host. He found him sitting in a comfortable room that was half-study half-lounge.

'This is a nice place you've got here,' he said. 'I never knew about this.'

'There are a lot of things you never knew,' interrupted the other. 'I always did believe in the old saying: 'Never let your right hand know what your left hand does'.'

'You certainly lived up to it,' retorted Fenner, pouring himself out a drink. 'But I want to hear the whole story. I don't think I ever got such a shock as when you turned up last night. How did the miracle happen?'

'There is no miracle. It is all very simple really.'

He began to speak, slowly at first, and then more rapidly, and Fenner listened in admiring astonishment.

'I see,' he commented when the other had finished. 'Well, I must say it was a cunning scheme. You might have told me, though.'

'I told nobody. These things are best kept as secret as possible. What would have been the use of going to all the trouble that I did, if I had spread it abroad?'

'Still, you might have told me,' grumbled Fenner. 'Look at the trouble it would have saved. We wouldn't have lost the emeralds if you hadn't been so close.'

'We haven't lost them. We have only mislaid them. It shouldn't be difficult to find that girl, and when we do — well, it will only be a little matter of persuasion to make her give them up.'

'I'll leave that to you,' said Fenner quickly. 'You can give me my share in cash, and I'll clear out. I'm too well known to the police to take any risks.'

'You'll get your share when the emeralds are recovered, and not before,' the other said coldly. 'I'm not paying out for something I haven't got.'

'It was your fault they were taken by this girl. If you hadn't been so almighty clever, and kept me in the dark, it wouldn't have happened.'

'Well, it has happened, and I'm not

going to argue about it. If you want your share, you'll have to help me get them back.'

An ugly expression came into the face of the man before him. 'Is that so?' he said softly. 'You'd better think again. If you don't part, I may have a nice little story to tell. What about that?'

'You can't squeal without giving yourself away. Don't be a fool!'

'I'm no fool. I should be if I listened to your suggestion. How do you know how long it'll take to find this girl? It may take months, and I'm not standing for it. If you don't pay me out my share at once, I'm going to take the risk and tell the police all I know.'

'Do you imagine I've got enough to be able to pay you, even if I was so inclined?' snarled his host. 'You must be mad! I haven't got the money available.'

'Then you'd better make it available,' broke in Fenner. 'Because what I've said I mean. For seven years I've kept my mouth shut, looking forward to coming out of prison and having a good time on the money that was due to me for those stones. And seven years is a long time. During that time you've been living at your ease in this house, and having the best of everything. I did the work, and I want the payment.'

'Otherwise you'll squeal, eh? Don't you realise, you fool, that last night made you an accessory to murder?'

'That was your idea,' Fenner muttered uneasily. 'I didn't want to do it — '

'Do you think anybody would believe that?' snapped the unknown. 'Use your brains, Fenner, if you've got any. You're as deep in this as I am. I'm willing to supply you with a certain amount of money, and let you stop here. But you've got to help me get those emeralds back. After that you can do as you choose.'

'What's your plan for getting them back?' asked Fenner, his previous truculence a little subdued.

'I haven't any plan at the moment. But that girl said her name was Trevor. I think she gave her real name, and if she did, we ought to be able to find her.'

'It'll be like looking for a needle in a haystack,' grumbled Fenner, going over to the window and staring gloomily down into the quiet street. The other man shrugged his shoulders.

'We'll find her, somehow,' he declared. 'You don't suppose I'm going to let those stones slip through my fingers, do you? We know what she's like, and we'll find her. She won't be able to dispose of them, and — '

A sudden suspicion flashed through Fenner's brain. The ease with which that girl had got away struck him now as being rather significant. The other was showing too much anxiety in his efforts to divert his, Fenner's, attention from his share of the emeralds. Supposing . . . ?

'Look here,' he snarled, 'I believe you know what that girl's up to. It would be a nice easy way of doing me out of my share to blame the disappearance of those stones on to her — when all the time she was working for you for about a third of the cut I should want!'

'Don't be a fool — '

'I'm not such a fool, either. It'd be easy for you to have her quietly hidden with the stones until you'd conveniently hedged me out of the way, and then to cash in and pull off a much larger slice for yourself. That's what I believe your game is. Why you — you!'

Fenner had been gradually working himself into a state that was almost hysterical. His own argument had convinced himself he was right, and the thought that he was being double-crossed now after the years he had waited brought his already tightly stretched nerves near to breaking point. With a sudden lightning movement, too quick for the other to intercept, he whipped out his gun and levelled it menacingly.

The unknown backed quickly, but his face showed no fear, only a cold fury that drew tight lines about his mouth.

'You blazing fool!' he snapped. 'I'd never seen that girl before in my life, and do you think for one minute I'd be crazy enough to take a slip of a kid like that into my confidence over a thing like this, a plan I've worked on for months? I tell you you're mad. Put that darn thing away and talk sense. Your confounded greed's got the better of you. Put that gun away!'

But Fenner was beyond reason. There was a queer, red light in his eyes and the unknown saw in a flash that words weren't going to stop him. A china ornament stood on a table by the unknown's hand, and with a quick wrist movement he snatched it up and flung it straight at Fenner's head, ducking as he did so.

The automatic spat viciously, but the bullet hummed harmlessly over the unknown's head, smashing its way through a picture that hung over the fireplace. In the same instant, Fenner staggered back as the ornament caught him across the forehead.

The unknown recovered quickly and, springing forward, brought his right fist round in a terrific blow that knocked Fenner, already off his balance, spinning across the room.

Then, in almost the same movement, it seemed, he sprang after Fenner and, straddling him as he sprawled on the floor, wrenched the gun away. He was panting with this sudden exertion to which he was obviously not used, but there was irresistible strength in the grip he fastened on Fenner's throat.

'Now,' he gasped, 'will you cut out this crazy nonsense and listen to me?' He spoke with slow deliberation. 'I do not know that girl. I have never seen her before. It is vital to me to get those emeralds back from her by any means I can. But I'll be damned if I'll pay you a red cent until I do get them back. Once they're in my possession you'll get your money, but not before. Do you understand?'

Fenner nodded dazedly. All the hysterical fire had died out of him and he was looking badly shaken. The cold anger in the other's eyes, the sharp clipped words, that terrible pressure on his throat, had changed him utterly.

The other eased his throat-hold and climbed to his feet, but as Fenner struggled upright he still held the automatic, covering him.

'Sorry,' Fenner whispered shakily, rubbing his throat. 'I guess I went mad for a moment. I thought you were double-crossing me, and after what I've been through — '

The other looked at him narrowly for a moment, and then thrust the gun into his pocket.

'All right,' he said. 'We'll forget about it. But start any more funny business, and you'll regret it. We've got too many important things to think about to start quarrelling. We've got to get after that girl.'

'That's right,' said Fenner, calm once more. 'We — ' He had moved towards the window and as he drew the curtains aside, he stiffened abruptly.

'There're two cars just stopped outside! Look — quick! There're several men getting out.'

With a muttered oath, the other was at his side.

Peering down into the street, he saw Fenner had spoken the truth. Two long cars had stopped at the kerb, and a number of men were alighting and staring up at the house.

'It's the police!' whispered Fenner, his face the colour of chalk. 'They've found us!'

'How could they have found us?'

snarled his companion. 'They couldn't have known — '

'Something must've gone wrong. What are we going to do? How can we get away?'

The other gripped his arm tightly.

'Pull yourself together,' he snapped, 'and come with me.'

He half-dragged the frightened Fenner across the room to the door.

'There's a way out through the garden.' He was hurrying his companion down the stairs. 'Pick up your hat and coat.'

Fenner seized them from the hallstand as they passed, and the other did the same. They had barely reached the dining room, the windows of which opened into the garden, when there came a loud and peremptory knocking on the front door.

'Quick!' whispered the unknown. 'This way!'

He threw open the french windows, and pushed Fenner through, closing them after him.

A path ran by the side of a lawn to a narrow belt of shrubbery, and along this they hurried, the terrified Fenner looking fearfully back over his shoulder

'Where does this lead to?' he asked breathlessly.

'There's a gate beyond the bushes which opens into a road. There are nearly always one or two cars standing there. My idea is to take one. If we can get a good start we may get away.'

They reached the gate, and jerking it open, passed through into a quiet street, before the sedate houses of which several unattended cars were standing.

'That'll do us,' said the unknown, after a quick glance, and made towards a black saloon, whose long bonnet suggested speed and power. His hand was on the handle of the door, when his shoulder was gripped and he was jerked back.

'I want you!' said a smooth voice quietly. He turned and his jaw dropped as he looked into the lean, sardonic face of Inspector Wedge.

'An unexpected meeting!' remarked the detective. 'We knew there was a back exit to the house, and we thought they might try it, so we decided to wait for you. This is the man, Elliot,' said Wedge, turning to

Inspector Elliot of G Division, who materialised out of the shadows. 'Mr. Elias Pringle, who is supposed to have died several weeks ago on Dartmoor but who is really very much alive. There will be several charges against him, but you can arrest him for attempted murder.'

'Good evenin', chums,' interposed a rich and fruity voice cheerfully from over Wedge's shoulder, and the huge bulk of Mr. Walker loomed into view. 'Not quite so warm as when we last met, is it?'

23

The skein unravelled

When Inspector Wedge recovered his senses it was to feel a cool wind blowing on his forehead. Opening his eyes, he stared up at the night sky, moonlit and star-spangled. Somewhere near there was a crackling sound, and he could see a ruddy light that danced and flickered eerily over the scrub and boulders of the open moor.

A face came between him and the sky — the anxious face of a girl.

'Oh!' said a voice softly. 'I'm glad you've come round.'

Wedge blinked up at her. His eyes smarted and his skin felt dry and painful.

'I had a dreadful job getting you out,' went on the girl. 'Your friend was able to help me, or I never should have managed it.'

'Wotcher, chum!' inquired the familiar

voice of Mr. Walker, a little more throaty and husky than usual. 'Ow're yer feelin', mate? I feels like a bit o' fried fish an' a pennorth o' chips meself. Lumme, it was a fine 'ow d'yer do, wasn't it?'

'It was nearly the last you bumped into, Walker,' croaked the detective. He looked at the girl. 'So you didn't go far, after all?'

'No,' she answered. 'I wanted them to think I'd gone, but I only drove a little way away, and then I stopped the car, hid it among some trees, and walked back.'

'Thank Heaven you did,' said Wedge fervently. 'You certainly saved our lives.'

'For which yours trooly thanks yer very kindly, miss,' said Mr. Walker. 'Lumme, but that's the warmest corner I've ever bin in — in more ways than one!'

Wedge scrambled to his feet. Except that he was a trifle shaky on his legs, he felt nearly normal.

'Can you drive us to Princetown, Miss Trevor?' he asked. 'I want to get on the telephone at once to Scotland Yard. If we hurry we may be able to catch Fenner and his friend before they can get very far.'

The girl agreed.

'Do you think you can walk as far as the car?' she asked, and Mr. Walker eyed him anxiously.

'I can walk all right,' said Wedge. 'Come on.'

The cottage was blazing furiously as they turned away. The detective saw in the moonlight the girl was dishevelled and her face was blackened. It had been very plucky of her to have ventured into that burning building and he said as much.

'I guessed what had happened when I saw those men leave,' she said. 'Luckily I had brought a knife back with me from the toolbox of the car. I thought it might come in handy as a weapon of sorts. Your friend was still conscious, and when I'd cut the ropes that bound him, he helped me with you. I wouldn't like the experience again, though,' she added with a shudder.

They reached the car and with Mr. Walker's bulk taking up most of the seat behind, they set off for Princetown. Had one of them chanced to glance behind they might have caught sight of the figure of a man who watched them depart. That man was Lang. Little did Wedge guess how near he was to one on whom he would have given a lot to lay his hands. He directed the girl at the wheel to stop at the police station. It didn't take them very long to do the journey, and almost before the girl had brought the car to a stop, Wedge was out and bounding up the steps of the station house.

He was gone for twenty minutes, and when he rejoined them there was an expression of satisfaction on his lean face.

'That's that,' he said. 'I don't think Fenner and the other man will get very far.'

'Wot do we do now, chum?' asked Mr. Walker.

'Get back to London as soon as we can. I mean to be there when we pinch Fenner and his friend!'

'S'right,' said Mr. Walker succinctly. 'You and me 'as gotter be in at the finish, ain't we?'

Which, as has already been described, they were.

★ ★ ★

Pringle and Fenner were taken to Scotland Yard. The description of them that Wedge had telephoned had resulted in their being traced to the house near Regent's Park by Elliot. He was justly proud of this smart piece of routine work, although the real person responsible had been a youthful constable in the district, who had recognised the description of Pringle that had been circulated as tallying with that of a certain 'Mr. Bates', living in a large house near the Park. He had seen 'Mr. Bates' arrive by car with a companion, who also matched the description of Fenner, and had immediately notified his inspector. That inspector had, in turn, passed the information on to the Yard and Inspector Elliot.

Pringle's identity was completed by the arrival of an agitated Miss Tillington, who gave one glance at him and fainted. When she recovered, she asserted without hesitation that he was her uncle, Elias Pringle.

Later that night Wyn Trevor told her

story to Inspector Wedge and Mr. Walker in the detective's office at Scotland Yard. She and Wedge smoked cigarettes, while the junkman sucked at a particularly disreputable pipe.

'I expect you've heard of James Trevor?' she began, and Wedge nodded.

'He used to be an inspector at the Yard,' he said. 'When he retired he set up as a private inquiry agent.'

'Yes,' said the girl. 'Well, I'm his daughter. When father started the business, I was at school, but when I grew up I begged him to let me help. After a lot of persuasion he did, and I was successful in one or two cases, carrying out investigations for the insurance company to see whether claims were genuine. And that's how we became mixed up with the Fullerton emeralds.

'When they were stolen, the firm who paid out the insurance money approached us, and offered us the job of trying to recover the stones. Their loss had been a huge one and they wanted to get it back if possible. The police had tried to trace the thief and failed, and they suggested father might be able to succeed, or at least find out what had happened to the emeralds. They were the insurance company's chief concern, and they were willing to pay a substantial reward to anyone who could get them back. Naturally this large sum made my father very keen. He tried all the known channels through which the stones might have been disposed of, but there was no trace of them. He came to the conclusion that the thief was holding on to them or the fence to whom he had sold them was, because they were too well known to be easy to get rid of.

'The police suspected the robbery had been carried out by Fenner, and my father agreed with this. We discussed the matter over and over again, and father came to the conclusion that the only faint chance of recovering the emeralds was to wait until Fenner came out of prison and keep him under observation. If he had stolen the emeralds, there was a pretty good chance that he would pick them up when he was free, or try to get into communication with the fence to whom he had sold them. Father was fairly certain he hadn't received payment for them, for the money would have been found when he'd been arrested.'

She paused for a second to tap the ash off her cigarette, and then went on:

'Unfortunately, the day before Fenner was due for release, father was taken ill and had to go into hospital for a serious operation. His long-cherished plan looked like falling through, because we had nobody who could undertake the job. Our business was not a large one, and nearly all our inquiries were personally conducted. Father suggested I should go to Scotland Yard, tell them what we had intended doing, and turn the matter over to them.'

'And as it's turned out,' interjected Wedge, 'you might have done worse than follow his advice.'

Wyn Trevor flashed him a smile.

'I know . . . But you see, that would have meant we should have to give up the reward, so without saying anything to father I decided to try to see what I could do.'

'Lumme, miss, that's wot I calls plucky

of yer orlright — and no error!' put in Mr. Walker.

'Well, to cut the story as short as possible, when Fenner came out of prison I kept him under observation. I had one of our men to relieve me, but mostly I did the job myself. I was following him on the night he met Ruccio and broke into your house, Mr. Walker.' She laughed a little. 'I thought then you might be the fence to whom he had sold the stones!'

'Wot, me a fence?' exclaimed Mr. Walker.

'That's what I thought at the time,' continued Wyn Trevor. 'I heard the shot, and saw Fenner come rushing out of the house, and wondered what had happened. Then, a light went on in the front room. I slipped in the gate and looked through the window. I could see Ruccio lying on the floor, and you bending over him, and I waited to see what would happen next. And then you fetched the aspidistra and seemed to be examining it. I jumped to the conclusion the emeralds were hidden in it, and when you had left the house, I got in by the window at the back. I was coming away with the plant when I ran into you coming back, and you snatched it out of my hands.'

'You didn't 'alf give yours trooly a turn neither.'

'It gave me a shock, too!' she confessed. 'I ran away, but I didn't go far, and when you were taken to the police station, I followed. I was convinced now that the plant contained a clue to the emeralds, and I determined to get hold of it. So the next morning I returned to Mr. Walker's house and — as you know — obtained the aspidistra by a trick.'

She stopped to crush out the stub of her cigarette in an ashtray.

'Wot I wants ter know,' Mr. Walker took the opportunity of asking, 'is wot told yer about that there stone in the fireplace at the cottage?'

'The aspidistra,' answered the girl with a smile. 'But it was only by accident! I examined the aspidistra when I got home, and there seemed to be nothing out of the ordinary about it. I stood it on a table, and then, wanting to put a tray on the table, I put the plant for a moment in the fender. There was a fire, and when I went to remove the aspidistra I was surprised to see some writing on one of the leaves.'

'Writin'? Lumme!' exclaimed the interested Mr. Walker.

'Something had been written on one of the leaves in a chemical which the heat of the fire had brought out,' explained the girl. 'It was a very short message, but quite enough. It just read: 'Under second stone. Hearth. Moor Cottage. Pringle.' You know the rest. I found out who Pringle was, and went to the cottage, where Fenner surprised me.'

Mr. Walker now turned to the detective.

'Wot I wants ter know next, chum,' he said, sucking noisily at his pipe, 'is 'ow did you find out about this bloke, Dingle, or Bingle — or wotever 'is name is?'

Inspector Wedge smiled across at him then at the girl, who was looking at him expectantly. He blew a cloud of cigarette smoke towards the ceiling.

'It's quite a simple story,' he began. 'For many years Fenner and Pringle worked in partnership. Pringle was the brains. He planned all the coups and disposed of the stolen property, while Fenner carried out his schemes. Pringle appeared, but kept in the background, and in case anything went wrong he evolved an ingenious and perpetual alibi. While he himself adopted the name of Bates and lived in London, he installed a man over whom he had a hold, in the cottage on Dartmoor under the name of Elias Pringle. This man — whose real name, by the way, was Eddie Ashton — became well-known in the district as an eccentric character, and even established his identity more thoroughly by employing a local firm of solicitors. All the stolen property was hidden in the cottage and sold from there by this false Pringle, acting under the instructions of the real one.'

'Lumme! Wot a game!' exclaimed Mr. Walker.

'It was a very clever game,' continued the detective, 'because it made the real Pringle practically completely safe. If there had been any trouble his alias would have been arrested and he would have suffered. After living for so many years as Pringle, Ashton would have had great difficulty in getting anyone to believe he was somebody else. And even if he eventually succeeded, the real Pringle would have had ample time to get clear away.'

Inspector Wedge paused to crush the stub of his cigarette into an ashtray. While he fitted a fresh one into his holder he proceeded.

'There was only one flaw in Pringle's scheme, and he knew it. This was that in the event of his dying suddenly — through an accident or something — his partner and confederate, Fenner, would have to know where the proceeds of any robbery which had been carried out between them could be found.'

He struck a match and lit his cigarette while Mr. Walker leaned forward with a question.

'Surely the other bloke, wot was pretendin' to be Pringle, could 'ave told him?'

Wedge shook his head.

'Ashton didn't know.'

He glanced across at Wyn Trevor and added:

'Neither did Fenner. Pringle trusted nobody. The cache under the fireplace was known only to himself. When he visited the cottage the man who was impersonating him was always sent away and he had no idea the cottage was used as a hiding place for stolen property.'

'He certainly had everything arranged pretty well,' interposed the girl.

'Yes, he was cunning enough . . . However, let's come to the Fullerton emeralds in which we are most interested.'

Wyn Trevor nodded.

'Pringle had had his eyes on these for a long time, and he planned with Fenner to get them. They were successful, but Fenner was arrested on another charge shortly after, and received a long sentence. Pringle had found difficulty in disposing of the emeralds. They were too well known. So he hid them in the cottage and waited until the hue and cry had died down. His idea was that later he would be able to find someone who would pay a big price for them and not ask too many questions.

'Time passed, and the day arrived when Fenner was released from prison. It was now that two things happened. Pringle was taken ill with influenza, and Ashton at the cottage died suddenly from a stroke. Fenner believing the real Pringle to be dead — he of course knew nothing of the impersonation — went to the cottage to find a clue to the whereabouts of the Fullerton emeralds. Pringle had told him this clue would be found with the aspidistra.

'When he arrived at the cottage, however, Fenner found it empty and its contents sent to Pringle's niece.'

Wedge turned to Walker and pointing at him with his cigarette holder, 'Well, now here's where you come in. Fenner, in urgent need of money, traced the aspidistra from Miss Tillington to you. He arranged with Tonio Ruccio to help him steal it from you. What happened in your sitting room that night is open to conjecture. Fenner says he promised Ruccio half the emeralds for his help.

When they found the aspidistra, Ruccio tried to double-cross him, and drew a gun. According to Fenner it was while he was wrenching it away from him that Ruccio got shot . . . However, that's for a jury to decide.'

'And I s'pose as 'ow this 'ere Pringle bloke when 'e got better from 'is influenza 'eard as 'ow this other chap was dead?'

Inspector Wedge nodded. 'Exactly,' he said. 'He hurried to the cottage after the emeralds and arrived on the same night as Fenner and,' — he turned to Wyn Trevor — 'you.'

'And the rest we all know,' the girl answered him.

'Not 'arf,' came from the junkman.

Inspector Wedge was about to add a comment when the telephone at his elbow jangled into life.

'Excuse me,' he said, and lifted the receiver. 'Hello?'

Mr. Walker and the girl were watching him and they saw the muscles of his jaw harden as his teeth clamped tight on his cigarette holder. They saw his eyes narrow as he pulled the telephone nearer, the better to speak into it.

'You're sure?' he snapped into the instrument. 'A village somewhere between Staines and Salisbury, eh? . . . Right, I'll be down there as soon as I can!'

He slammed down the receiver and there was a note of excitement in his voice as he turned to Mr. Walker.

'They've found the bicycle on which Lang escaped!'

'Lumme!' Mr. Walker gasped hoarsely. 'Where?'

'A village on the other side of Staines. Towards Salisbury.'

And Inspector Wedge picked up the internal telephone and began to snap instructions into it.

24

The storm

An hour after Lang had watched the car
— in which, though he was unaware of it,
were Inspector Wedge, Mr. Walker and
Wyn Trevor — disappear towards Tavistock, the storm broke over the moor. Quite
suddenly it seemed the clear moonlit sky
had clouded over from the west.

Lang had returned to his car a short
distance away from the blazing cottage.
He was sitting in it, undecided as to what
his next move would be when the rain
started to come down. With a muttered
curse he got out and struggled with the
hood. Like the car itself it was old and
rickety, but at last he managed to
manoeuvre it into position. There were
two or three tears in the material but it
would serve to keep off most of the rain
that was now descending more and more
heavily.

He got back into the machine and huddled behind the steering wheel, his coat collar turned up and his cap pulled over his eyes. The future looked hopeless and the downpour didn't help to heighten his spirits. It had been a crushing blow to have come such a great distance only to find it had been for nothing.

Lang had known that the man occupying the cottage was not in fact the real Elias Pringle. This discovery had come about in a curious way some months before when he, on holiday in the neighbourhood, had chanced to cross the moor. It was a hot day and having developed a thirst, and with no means of quenching it, he had, on passing the cottage stopped to ask for a drink of water. The man who opened the door to him he immediately recognised as a crook whom he knew by the name of Ashton.

This unexpected meeting had proved a great shock to the latter. Lang had instantly surmised there was something fishy in the man occupying a cottage in this desolate part of the world, and had determined to find out his secret.

The other, for his part, knew Lang was using his position as a police officer to mask his own criminal activities — the two had in fact in the past worked in co-operation.

During the conversation which had followed between the two men Ashton revealed he was being forced to impersonate a certain individual — Elias Pringle — who had a hold over him because of his criminal record. Ashton, however, was unable to tell the other the reason behind this deception, though not unnaturally, he was convinced it had some nefarious purpose. He begged Lang not to give him away for he feared Pringle's revenge. The other had promised to keep his counsel, though he had made up his mind there and then his knowledge would enable him to apply the thumbscrew on Ashton at some future time.

That time had come when he himself, hunted and desperate, had sought out the impersonator at the cottage as a means of escape. Ashton would hide him, get money for him, and when the opportunity presented itself, aid him to quit the country. That was what had been in Lang's mind when he, in his daring bid for freedom, had turned towards the west.

Now with bitter eyes he watched the rain beat against the windscreen in front of him. His petrol had run low and there was only enough left to carry him two or three more miles. This fact would have made it impossible for him to have followed the car he had seen driving away from the cottage which course had occurred to him. He wished he could have identified the car's occupant or occupants but he had only seen it from the back and it was too far away and moving too fast for him to do so.

He shifted his gaze to where the flames that had devoured the cottage were now being quenched by the storm. The thought struck him he would be able to discover whether or not the person or persons in the car had left anyone behind in the blaze, and if so it might be possible to find out whether it was Ashton or not.

He realised the man impersonating Elias Pringle was, if he still remained alive, his one source of hope. If he were dead he knew of no one else to whom he could turn for the help he needed in his attempt to escape.

He decided that as soon as the rain ceased he would return to the cottage and look round for evidence as to whether Ashton had been left to burn to death. He hoped fervently he would discover otherwise — not so much for Ashton's sake but for his own. Were he alive and it was he Lang had seen driving away, then at least there remained a chance of finding out where he had gone to.

The storm increased in violence. A strong wind drove the rain across the moor in fierce gusts. It hissed against the hood of the car, some of it finding a way in trickles through the holes that were torn in it. Lang cursed the rickety machine in which he was forced to sit and drew the collar of his coat closer under his ears.

Through the downpour he was able to make out the cottage. The fire had almost completely subsided and the walls stood black and crumbling against the storm, while a smoky vapour arose from the charred interior.

Impatiently Lang huddled in his seat and waited for the rain to stop. He was anxious to make his inspection of the ruin as soon as possible. He knew that on what he found there might depend his future and his life.

25

The Holdup

The storm continued for another half hour and then ceased as suddenly as it had began. The moment the rain diminished to a few spattering drops Lang got out of the car. He was stiff and cramped by his vigil, and the shoulders of his coat were wet where the rain had trickled through the hood.

He stamped his feet to restore the circulation through his limbs and, glancing round to make sure no one was in sight, he set off back to the cottage.

By the time he reached it the rain had stopped altogether. The moon reappeared from behind the fast disappearing mass of cloud and once again illumined the desolate moor.

He drew his coat collar about his neck and shivered. He seemed to see in those blackened, crumbling, ruins an omen of ill. Then he braced himself and with a resolute stride, swung up to the doorway that gaped, where the door was burnt to its hinges.

The place was a crumbling ruin. The floor above had fallen in, most of the roof with it, and the staircase was burned down. He stepped among the debris and searched as best he could in the fire-blackened mass for any trace of a human being. He found nothing. It seemed apparent the cottage had been left empty. It was very probable that the car he had seen drawing away from the blazing cottage had been driven by Ashton.

Where had he gone? There was no clue to be found so far as he could see.

As he quitted the charred and sodden ruin his attention was drawn to a shed at the end of the garden. This had completely escaped the blaze, and he approached it. The sight of a padlock barring entry aroused his interest. He wrenched at it and cursed as his clumsy efforts made no impression on it.

He searched round for an implement of

some sort, and next moment was grasping a short length of piping that had been thrown on a nearby rubbish heap. It did not take him very long to remove that obstinate padlock. Two savage jerks with the length of piping, using it as a lever, saw the lock and the staples that held it in place spring from the woodwork of the shed.

His foot smashed hard against the door, swinging it aside. He struck a match from a box he had found in the car, and his gaze searched the interior of the shed, adapting itself to the flickering gloom.

There wasn't much hope of him picking up a clue as to Ashton's destination he decided. It was a typical tool shed filled with gardening implements. Before the match spluttered out he discerned a heavy garden roller, a lawnmower and a dented watering can. He struck a second match. His eyes traveled over the odd collection of flowerpots, a jumble of withered plants, long forgotten, a rake and a hoe and a few cobwebs.

A grunt of disgust was leaving his lips

as he half turned. Then he caught a glimpse of something lying on the wooden shelf above him.

A third match proved it to be a suitcase, and a moment later he was hoisting the case to the ground

He cursed the rusty locks that at first defied his efforts. Cursed again as he broke a nail in the process of trying to spring back the catches, but persisted. Yet when the lid flew back nothing greeted his curious eyes save the frantic scurrying of a spider the glare of his third match had disturbed.

He let the suitcase fall and kicked it savagely. And it was that action which showed him the dim outlines of a label, stuck to one side of it. Again a match glow filtered the darkness. The label was scratched and the writing on it was almost undecipherable but he felt that here at last was something worthy of patience. Match after match flared up as he tried to make out the ill-formed characters written on that damaged label.

When Lang straightened himself he was muttering to himself like a child at school with a lesson to learn:

'Ashton . . . The Bungalow . . . Riverside Lane . . . Staines . . . '

Again and again he repeated the name and address. He smiled thinly. This must be Ashton's private address, where he lived before coming here to impersonate Pringle, for a certainty. He toyed with the theory and liked it. Yes, that was it. And it wouldn't surprise him, he thought, if Ashton wasn't at that moment already on the way to the bungalow.

He fingered his chin reflectively. He must follow. He must get to the bungalow. Then he remembered there wasn't enough petrol to take him more than three or four miles; certainly insufficient to make the long journey to Staines.

'I've got to get hold of another car,' he told himself.

He quitted the tool shed and walked back to where he had left the two-seater. With cold-blooded deliberation he laid his plans as he drove away from the moor. Making for the main road he chose a lonely spot and waited.

The road was not busy at that late hour, and he had to wait for close on thirty minutes before he saw the gleaming headlights of an approaching car. It was a powerful fast saloon.

Hoping there might be only one person in it he ran into the middle of the road and waved his hands. The oncoming machine had to stop, or else deliberately run him down. It stopped with a screeching of high-powered brakes.

'What's wrong?' the driver of the saloon poked his head out of the window. He was elderly and there was sympathy in his voice as he added: 'Breakdown? Anything I can do?'

With a grim smile Lang saw he was the only occupant. 'Thanks. If you will. Ignition trouble I think. It's so dark I can't . . .'

The other drew his car into the bank and climbed out.

'I've a torch here, if that's any help. 'Fraid I don't know much about cars,' he added.

'That's fine!'

Lang was grimly grateful for the

information. 'I wonder if you'd be good enough to hold the torch so's I can get a look at the ignition. Won't take a moment to put the thing right.'

The other man was eager to oblige. Switching on the electric torch he bent over the open bonnet of the car. Beside him rose the figure of Lang, straightening to full height. His right arm swung up viciously and then down again. The heavy spanner in his grasp crashed home on the Good Samaritan's skull. It was so unsuspected, so violently swift, that mercifully the man felt nothing. He collapsed, fanwise, over the bonnet of the car and lay still.

Lang's eyes were suddenly bloodshot and vicious. He held the spanner aloft again as if to make doubly certain that his victim was helpless, then changed his mind. Instead he flung away his weapon and, stooping, gathered up the unconscious man and carried him away into a deep gully that ran alongside the road.

He had everything cut and dried. Calmly he stripped his victim to his underclothes. Next he stripped himself, then redressed himself in the other's clothes and, in turn, dressed the unconscious figure in his garments. There were differences in the fit of the exchanged clothes, but beggars can't be choosers, he told himself grimly.

His victim's silk scarf made an admirable gag and with cruel thoroughness he tied it in place. A length of wire, taken from the toolbox of the car made an effective method of securing the man's wrists behind him. An odd strap, torn from the hood of the smaller car, served to bind his ankles.

'It'll be a few hours before he gets clear of that,' Lang congratulated himself. 'And if the luck's with me it'll be still longer before anyone comes across him.'

With easy strength he picked up his victim and dumped him in the small car. Then he steered broadside across the road, crashed through the hedge and drove on across a meadow until he reached a clump of trees. What better hiding place than this?

When he emerged from the thickness and darkness of that clump of trees he came on foot. His car with the bound and gagged figure of his victim dumped in it, had been abandoned.

There was no pity in his heart as he retraced his steps to the roadway. Whether the man he had left behind lived or died did not stir his conscience. He had been a means to an end, that was all.

The big grey saloon parked by the roadside offered him another stage in his violent bid for freedom. He grunted his satisfaction as he peered at the oil and petrol gauges. There was ample for his need.

Sitting at the wheel he now began an examination of the pocket contents of the suit of clothes he wore. In a leather wallet his exploring fingers counted a wad of crisp notes. The very touch of them sent a wave of pleasure surging through him. In the right hand trouser pocket he dragged out a handful of silver and copper coin.

The light from the dashboard allowed him to count the stolen money.

'Couldn't be better,' he smiled twistedly as he pressed the self-starter. 'I've money . . . a fast car . . . and a change of clothes. Now for Staines.'

He set the car moving forward, changed up into top gear and grunted again at the smooth performance of the engine. His gleaming headlights picked out the road that was to lead him at length to Staines and, at a steady speed, Lang sped along, well content with his night's work.

26

An unexpected meeting

Night driving has a sleepy effect on a fatigued man. As the miles flew under the rapid wheels of the saloon Lang found himself yawning constantly. He fought the impulse to fall asleep until his eyes read the time on the illuminated dashboard.

'Three o'clock. No wonder I could do with a sleep.'

He drove on now at a slower pace, looking for a quiet by-lane where he could pull up for a couple of hours. With the discovery he was tired now came an overpowering desire to eat. He felt famished.

There would be no opportunity of appeasing his ravenous appetite, however, until morning and, calling to mind that a cigarette or two will often sustain a hungry man he helped himself to the choice Virginian cigarettes he found in the gold cigarette case of the car's owner and smoked with nervous haste.

It was not until another twenty minutes had passed that he found the quiet by-lane he sought. He swung the grey saloon into it, drove along a distance of a quarter of a mile, and braked to standstill.

It was an ideal spot, seldom frequented, judging by the state of the ground surface, and almost completely shaded over with trees. He got out of the car to flex his cramped muscles, walked up and down smoking a final cigarette and then sprawled himself inside the back of the saloon under the luxurious warmth of a travelling rug.

The quietness and the darkness, for he had switched off his headlights, soon lulled him to sleep. His breathing became deep and regular, and a satisfied, triumphant smile masked his hard face as he slept.

The birds were singing in the trees when he awoke with a start. And their song told him he had slept longer than he had intended. With some alarm he leaned forward and peered at the clock on the dashboard.

'Nearly half-past seven . . . Still, I feel all the better for it.'

He stepped out into the roadway, began to throw his arms about to set the blood flowing in tune with the coldness of the morning air, then took his seat at the wheel. His eyes glowed suddenly as they saw the paper wrapper of a well-known firm of chocolate makers edging over the pocket flap in the offside door. A moment later he was devouring greedily the remaining contents of the packet. Presently he backed the car out of the lane, grimaced his pleasure at finding the road deserted and swung off towards Basingstoke.

It was a barber's shop past which he sped at forty miles an hour that reminded him he could do with a shave. Well, he could attend to that at the next village, for it was still rather early yet to find any shops open. Presently he found another quiet village. He coasted the saloon along looking for a barber's shop. The proprietor of the only hair-cutting establishment

in the place was just opening his door
when he drew up outside it.

'Top of the mornin' to you, sir,' smiled
the barber. 'You'll be my first customer, if
it's a shave or a haircut you're wanting.
This chair, sir, thank you, sir.'

The man was prepared to talk all the
while he worked, but he found his
customer uncommunicative.

'Come far, sir?'

Grunt.

'Hem! Nice weather for the time of the
year, sir.'

Grunt.

'What do you think of the political
situation, sir?'

Lang stirred himself then. 'Look here, I
came here for a shave. Get on with it, and
shut up!'

The other gave it up after that. Only
when he had sprayed and powdered the
blue chin of his customer did he speak
again, stating the price of the shave.

Lang paid him, then asked: 'Where can
I get a decent breakfast round here?'

'There's the Farmer's Arms, sir. That's
another mile along the village. I believe

they're open now. Bit early you know, sir . . . '

But Lang did not linger to hear more. He drove off at a burst of speed and garaged his car at the old Tudor inn that carried the swinging signboard 'Farmer's Arms'.

A sleepy-eyed woman was polishing the brass knocker on the door.

'You want breakfast, sir? What would you like? Egg and bacon — '

Lang cut her short with a gesture.

'I'd like a grilled steak and a kidney, if you can manage it,' he interrupted. 'Do your best. I'm famished. Yes, coffee and hot rolls . . . and plenty of butter.'

'Mercy be!' muttered the woman as she went off, for a steak and grilled kidney was an unusual breakfast order at the Farmer's Arms.

Lang permitted his harsh face a smile of appreciation when the woman came into the dining room some fifteen minutes later. The appetising odour of cooked meat and hot coffee permeated the small dining room.

'There you are, sir.'

He started in to wolf the breakfast at a speed that made the woman's eyes open wide with astonishment. But catching his glance of disapproval as he looked up suddenly, she hastily withdrew and proceeded with her polishing of the brass.

Lang felt a new man when that appetising breakfast had disappeared from his plate. He had washed and tidied himself whilst waiting for it to be cooked and now his confidence was at peak.

While he smoked a cigarette over his final cup of coffee he gazed at a map of the district that hung on the wall. He told himself it would be wise to skirt the village where he had left his bicycle in case anyone should recognise him. He could pass Salisbury on the left and approach Staines by way of Basingstoke.

With desperate confidence he took the wheel of the saloon and started off afresh. It was the sight of a blind man tramping the road towards him a few minutes later that suggested a pair of tinted glasses might afford him an additional disguise.

At a small chemist's shop outside Basingstoke he purchased a pair and grinned twistedly behind their dark shelter as he drove off again. He had nothing to fear now. No one would dream of looking for him in the vicinity of Staines. Not even if the owner of the car had been found and liberated, which he very much doubted, would the police think of looking for him in this part of the world.

He kept down the speed of the car now and the church clock was sonorously booming the hour of one when he entered Staines. A boy on a bicycle directed him towards Riverside Lane. It was in the residential part of the town, and, Lang discovered, led direct to the river.

He had no difficulty in locating the bungalow. It stood detached in a row of similarly built residences, with a well-laid-out garden on both sides. He brought the saloon to a standstill, switched off the engine and got down from the driving seat. No one seemed to be about as he walked boldly to the wooden gate and lifted the latch.

A short path took him to the front door of the bungalow. Without a tremor he rang the bell. Plainly to his ears came its shrill summons. Yet there were no answering footsteps. He thumbed the bell-push again. Still there was no response. Biting his lip he followed a pathway round to the back of the bungalow. Perhaps Ashton was sunning himself in the back garden.

There was no sign of him, however.

He tried the back door. It was locked and bolted.

He paused to review the position. As he saw it Ashton had not yet arrived, always assuming of course he was coming to the bungalow. Yet surely he would arrive some time. For where else might he go now the cottage on the moor had gone up in smoke? Next he thought of the car he had parked in the roadway outside the bungalow. Would it be safe to leave it there? He decided it would be as safe a place as any, for he jibbed at getting rid of that fast car. One never knew but it might prove a godsend if things went wrong.

Having turned this over in his mind he began to explore the back windows of the bungalow. A casual glance here and there told him if he chose to break in he would be unobserved by the occupants of the surrounding houses.

It did not take him long to break in. He wrapped a handkerchief round his right fist and plunged it straight at a window. The pane shattered under the impact and, by diving in his hand, he was easily able to spring the catch.

A moment later he was inside the bungalow and staring about him. The layer of dust on the mantelpiece told him the place had not been lived in recently.

He wandered from room to room and found solace in a half-empty bottle of whisky he discovered in the sideboard of the dining room. There was no syphon of soda, but whisky and water was better than no whisky at all. He poured himself out a half tumbler of the stuff. Then he flopped down on a comfortable settee with a replenished glass at his elbow and felt at ease with the world.

As he drank he surveyed the position afresh. By this time, he reckoned — familiar as he was with police methods — the abandoned bicycle would have been found. That would lead, of course, to the theft of the two-seater car. Obviously it would be from the inn, outside which the two-seater had been stolen, that the police would commence their enquiries. Probably they had already learned he had headed westwards.

On the other hand it was still likely they were not in possession of this information. In any case, he reckoned, he had smothered the trail. For surely the owner of the saloon car that even now stood outside the bungalow had not yet been able to give any alarm. Even allowing for a hitch in that supposition, it was unlikely the police would dream of looking for their man at Ashton's bungalow. For no one knew of his past association with the man who was impersonating Pringle. How could they?

No, he decided, the full power of the police enquiry would be centred on that area between the village where he had stolen the rickety two-seater and the coppice where he had left the owner of the second car he had stolen, bound and gagged in the first.

'They'll be wasting their time looking for me in that part of the world,' he assured himself, 'and all the time I'm sitting pretty here!'

He grimaced as he thought of Ashton. He was the man to help him. He would have to help him. If he refused there was that little matter of the impersonation of Elias Pringle. Under the threat of revealing the fact to Pringle that his confederate had revealed the secret of the impersonation to a third party, Ashton would do all in his power for his friend who was on the run.

'Sure, he'll help,' he muttered, sipping the whisky. 'I've got him where I want him — know how to turn on the screws if he's obstinate. It'll suit me nicely to lie low here for a few days . . . Let Ashton make all the arrangements for my getaway. Couldn't be better.'

He settled against the cushions of the settee. He was feeling drowsy again, and saw no reason why he shouldn't fill in the time of waiting for the other man's expected appearance by sleeping.

He decided to avail himself of one of

the comfortable beds in the adjoining rooms. They were made up.

He rose to his feet and stretched himself. Then he entered the best bedroom, tested the spring of the mattress and grinned his approval. He stripped to his underclothes, slithered between the clean sheets and was snoring before five minutes had ticked past.

He dreamed . . . the vaunting smile on his face said as much. He dreamed of freedom. He pictured Ashton frantically obeying his every whim and fancy. He was not to know that he, the man upon whom he relied so much was dead. Any more than he could foresee that in London Elias Pringle was soon to be apprehended by Inspector Wedge at the house in Regent's Park.

The hours ticked by. Thoughtfully, Lang had wound and set the clock going on the tiled mantel before turning in.

He could hardly credit the time when he awoke. The room was dark . . . very dark. The sudden glow of the electric light as he switched it on showed the hands of the clock pointing to the hour of ten. He dressed rapidly and leaving the front door of the bungalow on the latch decided to saunter out into the town for a meal.

It was the sight of the stolen car silhouetted against the night that brought a curse to his lips. What a fool he had been to sleep so long. No lights showed on the car. He was asking for a jealous policeman to do his duty.

Hastily Lang switched on the lights. He had been lucky. The less contact he made with the police the better it would suit him. He mooched away, head sunk on his chest, somewhat troubled now about that car.

Instinct told him to abandon it. For by now, likely as not, its owner had been found. The tell-tale number plates would set every policeman in the country on his track. Yet he liked the car. It was fast, in wonderful condition, and had a superstitious attraction for him.

If he abandoned it that would necessitate the stealing of another, for without a means of transport a fugitive from the law has precious little chance of prolonged freedom. He decided he would keep it a while longer.

It was only when he paused at a good-class restaurant he realised he had come without his dark tinted glasses. The reflection of his face in the large mirror that formed part of the decoration of the shop front told him that. He started nervously. What a fool he had been to leave those glasses in the bedroom of the bungalow.

He sped past the restaurant, seeking a place less well patronised. Along a narrow side road he found a café frequented by more humble folk. Cautiously he peered in through the window. Save for two waitresses the café was deserted.

He entered and sat down, giving the much-thumbed menu a casual glance.

'I'm hungry, miss!' he told the girl who came forward. 'I want something solid. None of your poached eggs and chip potatoes for me.'

'Would you care for roast lamb . . . and peas and new potatoes, sir?'

'Right. Quickly as you can.'

After he had eaten he smoked a

cigarette over a cup of coffee, glancing idly at a two-months-old magazine that he picked up from a neighbouring chair. He did not notice the swing doors of the café open. Neither was his attention disturbed from what he was reading until a shadow fell across the marble-top table and he looked up to see someone was taking the chair directly opposite him.

In a rich throaty, genial voice, the newcomer started to greet him.

'Good evenin', chum — '

Lang's blood turned to ice as he found himself staring into the round and rubicund face of Mr. Walker.

27

On the run

Mr. Walker had enjoyed the car run to the riverside town in company with Inspector Wedge. Outside the police station they had parted. It was the latter's intention, accompanied by the local police officers, to visit the village where Lang's abandoned bicycle had been found.

'I'll pick you up again at midnight, here at the police station,' Wedge had said. 'Unless you'd like to come along with me now?'

The junkman had hesitated. He would have liked to have been with the inspector, but deciding there were too many policemen going along with the Scotland Yard detective, and he would perhaps be in the way, he had shaken his head.

'S'orlright,' he had answered. 'I can amuse myself seein' the sights until you comes back.'

273

Thereafter Mr. Walker had ambled aimlessly about the town. He had stared at the river for a little while, and then turned his footsteps towards a café where he could have a 'nice cupper tea' and a sandwich.

Presently he had found one that seemed to suit his tastes, and his rubicund face had lit up at seeing a fellow-being within. To his way of thinking there wasn't much friendliness in wandering around a strange town. He was feeling a trifle lonely.

And so, with his characteristic desire to make himself at home and acquaint himself with the man who sat at the table reading as he drank his coffee, he had entered and proceeded to seat himself in the chair directly opposite him.

'Good evenin', chum — '

Then Mr. Walker's eyes had opened wide in astonishment, and he felt a prickling sensation run down the back of his scalp.

'Luv us!' he exclaimed involuntarily, as his eyes met those of Lang.

There was a split second between the

spoken word and what happened next. Then the other man acted. His hands gripped the marble-top table in the same moment as he rose to his feet. The table tilted suddenly, heavily. It crashed against Mr. Walker as he stood, half seated in his chair, knocking him flying. Long before the heavy table, with the junkman sprawling beneath it, crashed to the floor, the escaped murderer was darting towards the door.

'Stop 'im!'

That was all Mr. Walker had time to gasp before the falling table struck him a stunning blow on the head.

The two waitresses screamed. One of them ran towards the swing door as if to prevent the fugitive from leaving. The man snarled and swung a bunched fist at her. It caught her on the shoulder, spinning her round and sending her crashing against the counter.

'Help!'

The café proprietor rushed into the dining room, just in time to see Lang disappearing through the swing doors.

'What's happened?' he demanded.

'What's going on?'

'That customer, sir . . . that customer who came in just now for supper. He's gone!'

'What? You mean without paying his bill?' demanded the proprietor, his eyes popping with rage and dismay.

'Ye-es, sir. And he attacked that gentleman . . . ' continued the waitress pointing a trembling finger to where Mr. Walker was slowly picking himself up. 'Threw the table on him, sir.'

'And never paid his bill?' That seemed to be the other's chief anxiety. He raised his hands in horror. 'I'll send for the police!'

'Suppose you give a bloke an 'elpin' 'and . . . ? Thank yer, miss,' growled Mr. Walker as one of the waitresses pulled aside the heavy table. 'You won't believe me, mate, but the bloke wot's just 'opped it out of 'ere like greased lightning is an escaped murderer!'

The café proprietor gulped in such agitation that he dislodged his false teeth.

'A murderer? In my café? And never paid his bill? What's the world coming to?'

He yelled in an agony of fear as Mr. Walker started at a run towards the swing door.

'Hi! Have you paid your bill — '

'He hasn't ordered anything yet, sir,' said one of the waitresses, whereat the proprietor sat down heavily and mopped his brow.

Mr. Walker reached the street and peered up and down. But there was no sign of the fugitive. The darkness of Staines had swallowed him up completely.

Mr. Walker started off for the police station at as fast a pace as his bulk would allow. 'The 'ole bloomin' perlice force is lookin' for 'im and I bumps slap inter 'im in a perishin' café! Lumme! Wot an 'ow-d'yer-do!'

He was somewhat out of breath when he reached the police station and made his astonishing report to the sergeant in charge.

'Are you certain you weren't mistaken?'

Mr. Walker rubbed a bump on his head where the marble table had landed. 'I tell you it was 'im orl right, an' no error.

Better get on the blower ter Inspector Wedge, 'and't yer, mate? Arter all, 'e's 'andlin' this 'ere case, ain't 'e?'

The sergeant lost no more time. He 'phoned through to the police station in the little village whither Inspector Wedge and his colleagues had gone.

Meanwhile, while Mr. Walker waited patiently for Inspector Wedge to return, alternately smoking his disreputable pipe and rubbing his bruised head, Lang made his way back to the bungalow. The time between the junkman's breathless arrival at the police station and Wedge's return from the outlying village was to afford Lang a respite which was to mean all the difference between freedom and capture. He knew, as he looked back along the darkened streets of the town, after he had left the café, he had given Mr. Walker the slip. There was no sign of pursuit.

It was the car he needed now, he told himself grimly. Very soon the hue and cry would be raised. A cordon would be placed round the little town. Once that happened his hours of freedom would be numbered.

At a fast trot Lang reached Riverside Lane, turned down it and approached the bungalow. He thanked his lucky stars the powerful saloon car was awaiting him. And there was still ample petrol in it to take him miles away from Staines.

Suddenly he stopped dead in his tracks, and the breath whistled through his clenched teeth. Ahead of him a lamp post shed a radius of light which included that spot where he had left the saloon car outside the bungalow. And sharply framed in that radius was a uniformed figure!

At the same moment he saw the policeman the man was glancing into the driving seat. His next move was to open the garden gate and tramp heavily up the path.

An oath hissed from Lang's lips. Had he gone so far in his bold plan to be beaten now? The police constable was even at that moment ringing at the bungalow. What else could it mean but that he had come to arrest him — traced by some miraculous means to Ashton's bungalow?

How the police had been so swift, baffled him. He knew their routine methods from experience. He failed to see how his chance meeting with Mr. Walker could have brought such swift results. He stood there in the darkness trembling, a cold sweat breaking out over him. He saw now that the presence of Mr. Walker in the town suggested Inspector Wedge was not far away. But how came it his trail had been picked up so soon?

There was a muttered snarl of defiance as he swiftly made up his mind. He was getting out of Staines just as fast as he could. Let the police search Ashton's bungalow. Let them wait for him to return and pick up the car. They would wait in vain.

Pulling up his coat collar the fugitive retraced his steps along Riverside Lane back the way he had come and melted into the night shadows. He did not traverse any main streets. He was not such a fool as that. By a devious route, threading through quiet and deserted side streets, he eventually reached the main London road two miles outside the town.

London . . . That was the place to shelter him.

They would never think of looking again for him there. Hadn't he gone to such pains to get away from the city? Yes, London spelled a refuge for him . . . if he could reach it without attracting attention.

Merging with the shadow of a giant elm that grew a few yards from the highway, he waited. Car after car passed him, and he clenched his fists involuntarily till the nails bit into his palms as a police patrol car pulled in to the kerbside no more than ten yards from where he crouched.

He relaxed again when the patrol car resumed its way. Had they been looking for him, or had the mobile police just paused for a smoke, or to make a note of some motorist's misdemeanour? He did not know.

For half an hour he lingered in hiding waiting for the right type of vehicle to draw near. It was a lorry, or a tradesman's van he wanted. Then, to his intense relief he saw a dairy transport rumbling towards the big elm.

He stepped out into the road and raised his hand, and the driver of the milk lorry braked almost to walking pace.

'What's wrong?' queried the man at the wheel, staring down suspiciously at the fugitive.

'Give us a lift . . . I want to get to London . . .'

But the driver cut him short.

'Can't! Sorry! Against company's orders!' he replied curtly and took his foot off the brake.

'I'll give you this for your trouble!' yelled Lang, keeping abreast of the driver as the lorry crawled along, and flourishing a crisp treasury note.

The sight of that money overcame the man's scruples and his company's objections to their drivers giving strangers a lift. He stopped the lorry, and grinned.

'Jump up. Guess I don't mind obliging you.'

Lang scrambled up beside him and pressed the money into the driver's hand. Then he sat back, pressed hard against the woodwork of the driving cab, keeping himself, as well as he could, out of sight of other users of the road. He hardly spoke at all during the dreary, jolting slow journey, pretending to be asleep.

He was through with Ashton it seemed. No longer would the man be of any use to him now the police had traced him to the bungalow, its owner too would be suspected.

Meanwhile, the constable Lang had seen in the light of the street lamp was ringing the bell at the bungalow without result. He was not officially supposed to warn careless householders that if they left their valuable cars outside in the road all night they were asking for trouble. But that in fact was what this young, good-natured constable was doing, or intending to do.

Until, receiving no reply to his ring and knocks, and making his way to the back of the premises, he discovered a broken window. That discovery altered everything from the policeman's point of view.

28

Mr. Walker gets an idea

Police Constable Morton often hoped
something 'lively' would happen in the
vicinity of Staines. Failing that he hoped
for a transfer to another district, where
things did happen. From which it is not
hard to judge he was ambitious. The
neighbourhood was very respectable.
Barring one or two petty burglaries, a
very occasional 'drunk' and the theft of a
car or two, nothing very much happened
to brighten or cheer his ambitious
existence. In fact from his point of view
'business' at Staines was bad.

It had been sheer good nature on his
part that had prompted him to warn the
owner of the big grey saloon that he
might wake up in the morning and find it
gone. But when the young custodian of
the law discovered the bungalow was not
only empty but also showed traces of a

burglarious entry his most suspicious instincts were aroused.

He made a complete circuit of the bungalow, flashing his lamp into the various rooms. He noticed the broken window at the back, and again finally he came to the front door. The light from his lamp now showed him what he had missed before — the door was not properly closed. The locking device of the Yale had been thrust into position thus preventing the catch from closing in the socket.

Police Constable Morton reasoned that whoever had slipped the safety catch on the Yale lock had done so in order to facilitate his return to the bungalow. That meant the person was either without a key, or else it was someone with no right to be on the premises.

He rather thought the latter, as he remembered that broken window at the back of the bungalow. Then there was the presence of the high-powered saloon outside. Not unreasonably he connected the driver of the car with the person who had slipped the catch of the Yale lock.

He retraced his steps to the saloon and took out his pocketbook and started to lick the point of his stub of pencil. A moment more and the details of the car, including licence numbers and registration plates were written in indelible lead.

There was a 'phone in the bungalow — he could tell that from the overhead wires. As a police officer he had a right now to enter the place, having found the door open. Carefully he prowled into every room. He found no burglar, but there was evidence someone had been there fairly recently. The bed, for instance had been slept in. The clock on the mantel told the correct time, and it was only a twenty-four hour clock. Yet the other rooms all seemed to show the owner of the property hadn't been in the place for weeks, possibly months.

He picked up the telephone and asked for the local police station.

The desk-sergeant answered his call. 'Yes . . . Sergeant Broom speaking . . . 'Allo, is that you Morton? Anything wrong?'

Police Constable Morton told his

superior officer all he had discovered.

'Sounds a bit fishy,' was the sergeant's comment. 'Now let's 'ave that number again . . . '

Sergeant Broom broke off to smile a greeting as the door of the station opened to admit Detective. Inspector Wedge, followed by the local inspector and two or three other officers. In an aside the sergeant muttered to his inspector:

'Shan't be a second, sir. One of the constable's making a report.'

He took down the details of the registration and licence Police Constable Morton gave him on the pad before him.

'Right,' he said into the telephone. 'I'll send someone along to the bungalow. You'd better get on your beat.'

He rang off and turned to where Inspector Wedge was listening to Mr. Walker's description of all that had happened between him and Lang in the café.

'Humph,' murmured Wedge, lighting the cigarette in his long holder, 'Lang's been doubling backwards and forwards in an astonishing way. While we were at the village the news came through from Scotland Yard that the two-seater he'd stolen was picked up in a field — hidden among the trees — not far from Tavistock.'

'Tavistock?' whistled Mr. Walker. 'Wot was 'e doin' down there?'

The other shrugged. 'And that's not all,' he went on without answering the junkman's question. 'In the car was an elderly man, bound hand and foot. Been there for hours.'

'Lumme!'

'It appears Lang stopped this man on the road and asked for help with his car — the two-seater he'd stolen. The man got out of his big saloon, and all he had for his trouble was a crack on the head, the loss of his clothes, his wallet, gold cigarette case and his valuable car into the bargain.'

''Ard luck for 'im,' commented Mr. Walker sympathetically. 'Then I suppose Lang 'opped orf in his car and came down 'ere?'

The Scotland Yard man nodded.

'Well, chum, if you knows the number

288

it shouldn't be difficult to cop 'im. Can't be very far away from 'ere, can 'e?'

'We've got the number all right.'

Inspector Wedge turned to the local inspector. 'Better radio the patrol cars, hadn't you? Tell 'em to stop driver of grey saloon . . .'

The mouth of Sergeant Broom gaped wide when Inspector Wedge added the number.

'That — that number, sir,' he gulped, jabbing his writing pad. 'It's here . . .'

'Eh?'

'Constable Morton just 'phoned me about a car that's been left outside a bungalow in Riverside Lane.'

Inspector Wedge's black eyebrows met over his narrowed eyes. 'So that's where he was hanging out?' He turned to the others. 'Come on! The sooner we're on the spot the better.' He included Mr. Walker in his gaze. 'You come along as well.'

'Anythink to oblige, chum, that's me all over!'

In a few minutes the fast police car had pulled up outside the deserted bungalow.

Police Constable Morton returning on his beat was in time to greet his superior officers smartly and tell them all he knew.

'It's the stolen car all right,' snapped Inspector Wedge, checking up on the licence disc and number plates. 'But what's it doing here? Why did Lang come here? Let's have a fingerprint expert along,' he said to the local inspector. 'We'll soon see if it's our man who's been inside the bungalow.'

While a policeman dashed back in a car to the police station to pick up the required expert, Inspector Wedge, followed by the others including Mr. Walker entered the bungalow.

Within ten minutes a fingerprint specialist had arrived and was at work. Even without photographs he was able to declare the prints he had found were those of the wanted man.

'I know 'em with my shut eyes,' he asserted. 'They're in evidence everywhere. On the whisky bottle — the glass — the clock — the handles of the door . . . '

'Right,' murmured Inspector Wedge,

'I'll take your word for it. Lang's been here, but I don't think he'll come back.'

'Not blinkin' likely!' put in Mr. Walker. '' E *would* be a mug. But don't 'is comin' 'ere suggest 'e might 'ave a chum, like? Arter all, it's a long way from Tavistock, and a feller wouldn't do a journey like that just on the chance, would 'e now?''

Wedge nodded in agreement.

'Find out who owns this place,' he said to the sergeant at his elbow.

While they went about their appointed tasks, Mr. Walker found himself a comfortable armchair and stretched himself at ease. He watched the activity around him with a benign expression on his round face. By this time he was getting accustomed to police procedure. There was nothing new to him now in the business of taking photographs of a wanted man's fingerprints. There was nothing very novel in listening to Inspector Wedge, while the Scotland Yard detective put through a telephone call asking for a general radio message to be flashed out warning the police of all

291

counties to keep a lookout for the wanted man.

Only when a constable who had been examining the contents of a drawer in one of the rooms discovered an addressed envelope did Mr. Walker allow his interest to soar.

'This looks as if it's addressed to the tenant here, sir,' the policeman told Wedge. 'Ashton's the name.'

He was interrupted by the Scotland Yard detective suddenly grabbing the envelope from him with an exclamation.

Quickly Wedge glanced at it — 'Eddie Ashton' he saw through his cloud of cigarette smoke as he read.

'That was the name of the bloke wot pretended to be Pringle, ain't it?' said Mr. Walker. 'And wot's dead . . . '

Inspector Wedge nodded absently. He was piecing together the fragments of the jigsaw puzzle picture of Lang's journey as he saw it. The escaped murderer had not only known Ashton, but, it seemed highly probable, had been aware he was impersonating Elias Pringle and living at the cottage on the moor. That accounted for his visit to the vicinity of Tavistock. He had found the cottage either empty, or had discovered it was occupied by Inspector Wedge himself, Mr. Walker, Wyn Trevor — to say nothing of the real Elias Pringle and Fenner during their brief stay there — or he had arrived afterwards when the place was ablaze. It was all according to the hour he had reached the moor.

Anyway Ashton had not been there to greet him as expected. Lang had then decided to seek him at this bungalow, where he knew he lived under his own name.

That, the detective was satisfied, presented a fairly accurate array of the facts. The question arose, where was the fugitive now? Wedge gave the local police a précis of what he thought had been Lang's activities, and Mr. Walker listened to him, marvelling at his cold, logical piecing together of the puzzle.

He offered the suggestion that their quarry had turned back in the direction of London. The local inspector snorted his disbelief of such a theory. But Wedge regarded the junkman with interest.

'What makes you say that, Walker?' he queried gently.

'Where else can 'e go to? 'E's drawn a blank down at 'is pal's cottage on the moor, and 'e knows it's too dangerous ter 'ang around these parts. Staines ain't big enough.'

Inspector Wedge nodded his domed head slowly in agreement. The junkman, encouraged, proceeded:

' 'E'll choose a big place to 'ide out in, and where better'n good old London?'

'I agree,' said Wedge.

'In any case,' continued Mr. Walker, 'I oughter be a-goin' back there. I got my business to attend to.'

After a few more moments of discussion, a move was made back to the police station. A policeman was left at the bungalow, and the stolen car taken to the station yard.

Mr. Walker looked at the clock on the station wall as they entered, and stifled a yawn. It was close on two o'clock.

Soon a police car was ready for him and the Scotland Yard man, to take them back to London. The junkman settled himself comfortably in the back seat, and Inspector Wedge climbed in alongside him, and the car roared off.

It was only when he asked Mr. Walker a direct question that he made the discovery he was fast asleep. Inspector Wedge realised the futility of a one-sided conversation, and sat back to smoke silently.

After a while a deep rumbling snore proceeded from Mr. Walker.

That was too much for the detective. He closed his eyes . . . his long cigarette holder drooped and fell to the floor, the cigarette going out.

Soon sonorous rumblings of two tired men who were sleeping with their mouths wide open came from the back of the speeding car.

29

At the sign of the Waterfront Club

'How far d'yer want to go?'

Lang did not seem to hear the lorry driver's enquiry. He sat huddled against the wall of the driving cab, his eyes closed. His thoughts were not focused on things around him. The driver nudged him with his elbow.

'You asleep? . . . Oh, you're not. I said how far d'yer want to go?'

Lang shook himself. 'Oh — er — anywhere near London,' he said quickly.

The lorry rumbled on into the night, and the fugitive allowed his imagination full play upon the future again. He had no real destination in mind. He had counted on Ashton's help. Now that he was dismissed from his scheme of things someone had got to help him. Who, out of all the people he knew, could he turn to now?

One by one he martialled before his mind those whom he could call his friends. One by one he dismissed them, either on the score he could not trust them not to betray him, or the lack of financial resources. It was someone with money, someone with facilities for helping him to escape from the country he sought.

Then suddenly he remembered the existence of Max Gartell.

His bloodshot eyes gleamed with a new hope. Max Gartell was rich and, in the sphere wherein he moved, powerful. He was not exactly a friend of his, but he came into the category of an acquaintance. In the past Lang had rendered the flashy owner of the 'Waterfront Club' several services. True he had been bribed in return, for those services had occurred when he had been stationed at Commercial Road.

He had known then Gartell was a dope runner. He had unearthed ample evidence that the 'Waterfront Club', which was an old disused wharf on the Thames waterfront, cloaked Gartell's illicit trade.

Outwardly the place was a nightclub where the more notorious of Mayfair's bright young things, and the more elegant members of the upper crust of the underworld foregathered. The incongruity of this luxurious night-haunt in its squalid surroundings had appealed strongly to the sort of people it was designed for. Not the least of its attractions was the fact that those unfortunates who craved for drugs could here satisfy their longings — at a fat price.

And so Gartell prospered. Gradually he had built up an organisation whose ramifications were a thorn in the side of the police. From the 'Waterfront Club' the drug-czar controlled his agents, satisfied his 'clients', paid his underlings well and showed to the inquisitive outside world nothing but the appearance of being a genial night-club proprietor.

Lang wondered why he hadn't thought of him before. The man knew a number of sea captains and ships' officers, for these were necessary links in his chain of contact. For one who was bent on fleeing the country such people could be of invaluable assistance.

Lang's smile slowly faded. It came home to him he would have to throw himself on Max Gartell's mercy, not at all a pleasant reflection. In the old days it had been Lang who held the power. And he had made the dope-peddler pay for it accordingly. It would be different now, however. The positions were completely reversed. Somehow he did not relish the thought.

He shrugged and dismissed his qualms. A man wanted for murder couldn't afford to be squeamish.

It was when the lorry was rattling through Aldgate that Lang asked to be set down. He walked swiftly away in search of a taxicab, and when he eventually found one, directed it to a destination that would set him down within three hundred yards of the 'Waterfront Club'.

Arrived at his destination, he paid off the taxi and continued his way on foot.

The last stage of his journey took him along a dark, cobbled alley. At the end of it was a door, above which hung an illuminated sign, which bore the legend

'WATERFRONT CLUB'. The number of expensive cars parked outside told him there was a good attendance, as usual, and he pushed open the door and climbed the flight of wide stairs.

At the top of the dark staircase his further progress was barred by another door, heavy and iron-studded. In response to his ring at the bell a grille, slotted in the upper half of the door, opened. Hard enquiring eyes surveyed him.

'What do you want?'

'I want to see Mr. Gartell. I'm a — a — friend of his. It's very important business.'

'Your name, please?'

'Never mind about my name,' snapped Lang. 'Tell him I want to see him.'

The grille slid home again. Lang waited impatiently while the minutes ticked by then he tensed as the big, heavy door was opened to him and he was invited to enter.

'This way . . . '

He found himself in a luxuriously furnished vestibule, cunningly illuminated with concealed lights that shed a rich warm glow over the place. At the far end of the vestibule was the curtained entrance to the club restaurant and dance floor and as he followed at the heels of the doorman the soft strains of dance music filled his ears.

'This way,' said his guide, turning off to the left before the restaurant was reached. 'Mr. Gartell is in his office.'

He halted before a mahogany door and tapped respectfully on the panels. A voice within invited entry, and a moment later Lang found himself face to face with Max Gartell.

30

The dope-czar

For a few seconds there was complete silence in the room. Then the squat, bloated-looking proprietor of the nightclub grinned. The immediate effect was to render his already piggy eyes into nothing much more than flashing slits set between folds of flesh. The wreathing smoke issuing from the enormous cigar he held in his podgy bejewelled fingers added to the grotesque effect he produced

'Well, well . . . '

Gartell's silky purr expressed wellfeigned pleasure. 'If this isn't a surprise! Fancy you turning up here.' He became aware of the doorman who lingered unnecessarily, and dismissed him with a wave of his be-ringed hand.

'Sit down, my dear fellow. Sit down!'

The visitor dragged forward a chair and sank into it. Deliberately the other jerked up the lapel of his flashily cut evening jacket and sniffed at the expensive purple carnation threaded into the buttonhole. Then setting it back in place, he beamed at his visitor.

'Never thought I'd be honoured in such a fashion. Mr. Lang, the escaped murderer, walks into my parlour.' He pawed his double chin reflectively. 'Sometimes, it's hard for a law-abiding citizen to do his duty. Yet you know it *is* my duty, of course, my dear fellow, to send at once for the police . . . eh?'

'You wouldn't do that, Max? I've been a good pal to you in the past.'

'A good pal, eh?' smirked Gartell. 'One way of looking at it, I suppose. But you were a damned bad policeman though, weren't you? You took the public's money for upholding their laws, and you took mine for breaking 'em.'

'I want help, Max. I've got to get out of the country — ' Lang was beginning, when suddenly the other rose from his chair quietly and padded across the thick carpet to the door.

He opened it with a sudden, swift

action, and his piggy eyes smouldered. In the corridor outside just stooping to pick up a handkerchief was the man who had admitted Lang into the club. That he had been listening outside the door, it did not need a master mind to see.

'Listening in, eh?' sneered Gartell.

'I — I — dropped my handkerchief — and came back for it,' the eavesdropper excused himself guiltily.

'Well, get the hell out of here,' purred Gartell, a dangerous inflection in his voice. 'I like keyhole listeners as much as a cat likes poison!'

The other moved off, and Gartell slammed the door. Chewing at his cigar he returned to his desk. Momentarily oblivious of Lang he pressed a button at his elbow and a moment or so later a shifty-eyed individual, pale-faced and with a cigarette stuck in the corner of his mouth, entered.

'Nick,' said the drug-trafficker to the newcomer, 'I got a feeling about that Hass fellow. Caught him listening at my door a moment ago . . . and that's not the first time. Keep your eye on him, will you? We don't want a squealer round here.'

A cruel smile curved the thin lips of Nick the Snake. He winked expressively and threw back a reply without removing the butt end of the cigarette from his upper lip.

'I get you. Leave Hass to me.'

He withdrew silently, without once looking in the direction of the other man, and closed the door softly behind him.

'Now, what were we saying?' The flashy proprietor was all smiles again, as he addressed Lang.

The latter realised Gartell was playing with him. The man knew well enough why he had paid him this visit yet it seemed to appeal to Gartell's twisted sense of humour to hear him repeat his appeal for assistance.

'I said I want your help, Max. I've got to clear out of the country.'

'Sure, sure,' murmured the other, smiling. 'Myself, well I never experienced what it's like to feel a rope round my neck, but I can understand how you feel. Take it easy . . . have a cigar.'

And his fat bejewelled hand gestured towards the box of expensive Havanas before he eased his podgy squat figure back into the depths of his armchair.

It did not take Lang long to tell him what he intended.

'You're the only one I can turn to,' he concluded. 'I thought — I thought, for old time's sake, you'd — you'd — help me . . . ' His voice trailed off.

There was a full minute's silence before Max Gartell spoke. A frown darkened his podgy, dead white face. His thick lips moved restlessly over the end of his cigar. Then he leaned forward and the crafty, ingratiating smile returned.

'You know, I'm inclined to help you,' he remarked lightly. 'In my — er — business one has to use a sea captain or two.' He winked knowingly. 'Well, I've got a small boat lying down the river, with a captain aboard who does what I say without question. He's due to sail tomorrow to a quiet little port on the continent . . . On — er — business,' he added with a leering chuckle.

Lang nodded and waited expectantly.

He could scarcely believe in his good fortune.

'I can fix it to have you put aboard,' the other was saying, rubbing his chin reflectively. 'The skipper'll see to it you're smuggled ashore when he reaches port. I can fix up a passport for you, too.' He looked at the end of his cigar, adding: 'I'll be generous and give you enough money to start you off on your new life . . . Well, how does that appeal to you?'

The other's eyes glistened.

'Fine, Max! My God, I never thought . . . '

He was interrupted by a curt gesture of the podgy hand.

'Good . . . But wait a minute. I haven't finished yet. I'll do all this for you, if you'll do something for me in return.'

'Name it!' came the swift response.

The piggy eyes of Max Gartell roved questioningly over the harassed face of the other man opposite him.

'Ever heard of Lee Burke?'

Lang thought for a moment, then replied:

'Runs a rival dope racket to yours, doesn't he? Makes out he's an artist, and

307

has got a studio in Chelsea. If I remember right, he chucks his dough about on eccentric parties and all that sort of crazy stuff . . . Yes, I know Lee Burke. The police have had their eyes on him for a long time. Too smart for them, though . . . He's nearly as smart as you . . . '

'Ah!' It was a hissing exclamation, and looking up Lang saw a diabolical expression take command of that bloated, fleshy face. 'Nearly as smart — as you say.' He banged his fist on his desk. 'He's spoiling my business! He's cutting in on me . . . I went as far as offering to buy him out, but the swine turned it down. I dropped my pride and offered to go fifty-fifty with him, merging the two businesses into one. He told me to get to hell out of it. I haven't forgotten that. By God, I haven't!'

Again Gartell smashed his podgy fist down on the desk. A slow smile came over Lang's face.

'Why don't you get one of your boys to — er — eliminate him?'

'I don't like violence,' Gartell purred. 'Besides, if I get a job like that done, the man I hire to do the croaking might be apt to turn on me later, and try to blackmail me . . . Or he might squeal to the police. No, I like to keep my business clean, see.' He paused and his piggy eyes bored into the other man's face. 'But with you, it's different . . . '

'How d'you mean?'

'Well, you're already booked for the eight o'clock walk if they get you. Another murder can't make it much worse, eh? And,' he added, smiling thinly, 'you'll never be tempted to open *your* mouth, will you? I'd have nothing to fear from you.'

A long whistling breath left Lang's lips.

'You mean, you want me to silence Lee Burke? In return you'll fix me a passage to the continent, give me a passport and enough cash to find my feet?'

'That's the deal,' smiled Max Gartell. 'The job'll be easy. As soon as you've fixed it, you can nip aboard my boat and — fade.'

Lang was silent.

'Well . . . that's my proposition,' purred Max Gartell. 'Take it or leave it.'

George Hass was a poor actor. His
flushed face and the nervous twitching of
his eyes spoke eloquently of some
emotion raging within him that he found
difficult to suppress.

There was good reason for it. He had
recognized Lang, as the police officer who
had visited the club in the past. He knew
from the newspaper reports he was now
an escaped murderer on the run.

The discovery had set a wild rush of
thoughts coursing through his brain. He
was not a bad fellow at heart. His early
days had been spent in poverty and he
had fallen in with a flashy set of young
men who considered crime more profit-
able than honest work. That had been the
beginning of Hass' downfall. It was an
easy step from petty thieving to house-
breaking. And then the inevitable had
happened. The police had picked him up,
knocked his alibi sky-high and found the
proceeds of a robbery hidden in his
bed-sitting room.

For three years, in the grim confines of

Dartmoor he had ample time to repent. He came out into the world again a reformed character. Honesty, thenceforth, was to be his guiding principle.

The stars, however, were against him and his desire to reform. He found no honest work to do. People didn't want an ex-convict in their employ. It was the same everywhere he tried to find employment. Somehow it seemed his past arrived at any prospective place ahead of him.

He did not tumble to things until he found himself under the patronage of Gartell. It was the wily dope czar who had informed the people to whom Hass had applied for work that he was an ex-convict. For Gartell had marked him down for himself.

The job of doorman at the Waterfront Club had been given to him when he was in the mood to commit suicide. At the time the offer of work came to him like a gift from heaven. But it was only a job to screen others of less lawful purpose.

Within a short while Hass was deep in the toils, an unwilling helper in the unholy traffic of drugs. However, he had a philosophical turn of mind, and until he met Marjorie Collins he had been prepared to spend the rest of his days in the service of Max Gartell.

The advent of Marjorie, however, began to change his views. She was a good kid, straight and very honest. With a woman's shrewdness she discovered the real business that went on at the Waterfront Club and begged her sweetheart to get out of it as quickly as he could.

But that was easier said than done. Hass would gladly have given notice to his fat employer. But, he had a horrible fear deep down within him that once he was free of Gartell something tragic would happen to him. He knew too much . . . and those in the employ of the dope trafficker who knew too much had a nasty habit of meeting with fatal accidents when they showed signs of reform.

'All in good time, Marjorie,' he had told her. 'Then we'll get married and — and . . .'

It had ended there. Hass was too

terrified to take the step into matrimony, which would lead him away from the Waterfront Club. He had a conviction such a step would land him in the grave, a knife or a bullet in the back.

The coming of Lang to the Waterfront Club however, changed matters considerably. At least, that was the way Hass regarded it. Max Gartell knew the man was an escaped murderer. He was harbouring him, when his plain duty was to hand him over to Scotland Yard. If the police knew the facts there would be a stiff prison sentence for the nightclub proprietor. Once he was safe behind bars the dope-ring he controlled would be revealed, and a further number of years' imprisonment added to his sentence.

Once he was out of the way Hass felt he would no longer have anything to fear. He was the master mind, the schemer, the Big Boss who issued the orders. The rest were nothing, some not unlike Hass himself, unwilling servants.

As he carried out his duties at the heavy, grille-fitted door he turned the problem over in his mind again and again. He knew he would have to proceed with extreme caution. Already he guessed Gartell suspected him of eavesdropping.

'I daren't go straight to the police,' he told himself. 'I daren't. That would be too obvious. I'll have to pass on what I know to someone else, and let them inform the police.'

But it was not until the musical clock in the vestibule struck the hour of three in the morning that a brainwave occurred to him.

'I've got it. Mr. Walker! He'd help me. Yes, he's the chap. Why didn't I think of it before?'

He began to feel much easier in his mind at the thought of confiding his troubles to the philosophical junkman. He had already met him several times round a dartboard or over a half-pint at the little public house which both frequented. The club would close at four o'clock, and he would be off duty. Time for him to have a short sleep in his bedsitting room off the Commercial Road, breakfast and a clean up, before seeking out his friend in need.

31

Mr. Walker mends his barrow

Mr. Walker counted out eight rashers of bacon and dropped them into his frying pan. He followed them with two new-laid eggs and a large piece of bread, which he fried in the bacon fat. When all was ready he sat down to his breakfast. The meal over and washed down with copious draughts of strong tea he felt he had done himself justice.

He had risen late that morning, for in company with Inspector Wedge, he had arrived back in London when the fingers of dawn were lifting the curtain of night from the sleeping city. After he had said his farewells to his friend he had made his way back to his little house in Commercial Road.

The clock was striking ten when he rose from his breakfast table. He sat back in his chair, eased the buckle of his belt a point or two and groped for his old pipe. Having charged it with the particularly strong brand of tobacco to which he was addicted, he sat awhile ruminating before the kitchen fire.

Well, he was little the worse for the exciting adventures in which he had been involved, since the momentous occasion three nights ago when Inspector Elliot of G Division had detained him, following the murder of Tonio Ruccio.

Then his thoughts swung back to the day's work ahead of him. It occurred to him he might make a start by overhauling his junk-barrow. It was a very old affair, and in danger of collapsing at any moment. Odd bits of wire and rope held it together at its weakest points, but the philosophical Mr. Walker remained quite unperturbed by its rickety appearance and danger of imminent collapse.

Even he, however, was beginning to admit it was really necessary to do something about the near-side wheel. Two of the spokes were missing and it seemed imperative that some support should be put in their place.

And so presently, after he had tidied up the house, he wandered out into the little back yard. He entered the shed wherein was stored the profusion of junk, ranging from old bicycle wheels to a battered cuckoo clock. At length, his questing eye came upon an old chair that had two legs missing. Mr. Walker considered that the remaining legs, with a little careful contrivance, would do admirably to replace the spokes in the wheel of his barrow.

He set to work at a leisurely pace with saw, hammer and nails. And as he laboured the events of the past few days began again to flash across his mind in a panoramic strip of thrills.

Starting off with the murder of Old Cartwright in the jeweller's shop, there had followed the exciting adventures he had encountered with his old friend Inspector Wedge of Scotland Yard . . .

'Really,' Mr. Walker muttered to himself, as he carefully fitted the first improvised spoke in the wheel of his barrow, 'I seem ter 'ave been 'opping abart from 'ere to there without stopping ter take a breath!'

As he set about adjusting the second spoke he began to wonder whether there was any further news about Lang. Maybe they would be able to tell him something at the Commercial Road police station. He decided when he had finished this job he would amble down there and have a chat with the officer on duty.

His ruminating was interrupted by a tap at the door of his shed. Hammer in hand he opened it, and his rubicund face broke into a smile of welcome as he recognised the caller as George Hass.

'Good mornin', chum.'

'Can I come in for a while, Mr. Walker?' said the visitor and the junkman noticed he seemed a trifle strung-up and excited. 'Got a bit of a problem, I have, and I thought maybe you might help me.'

'Well, come in, anythink ter oblige, that's me all over.' And indicating the chair from which he had just removed the legs, Mr. Walker placed it on top of an empty packing case and with a chuckle invited the other to sit down.

'There y'are, chum — take it easy. I

dunno wot you've got on yer mind, but wotever it is get it orf yer chest, an' we'll see wot it's all about. Don't take no notice of me, I can work an' listen.'

Hass perched himself on the improvised chair and nervously lighting a cigarette, began to talk. He made a clean breast of his past and then told the story of how he had come to be employed at the Waterfront Club. Mr. Walker paused now and again in his work to look up with an encouraging word or a smile as the other talked.

'And then, early this morning, this happened,' he wound up. 'That chap Lang turned up at the club and I — '

The mention of that familiar name came as such a shock to Mr. Walker that the heavy hammer blow aimed at a nail which was holding the second spoke in place missed its target completely and landed on his thumb.

'Say that again, chum,' he muttered sucking at the damaged member.

Hass obeyed, little dreaming of the other's interest in the escaped murderer's activities.

'Oh, it was him all right. I've seen him when he used to come to the club before — there's no mistake. Now he's come to ask Gartell for help . . . and I've the feeling he'll get it, too . . .'

'Lumme!' exclaimed the junkman, so astonished by what he had just heard, he scarcely realised the burning pain in his thumb.

'You see,' added Hass in a burst of confidence. 'I've been wanting to get clear of Gartell for a long time.' He hesitated. Then:

'I — I've got a girl, and — ' he stammered, and Mr. Walker stopped sucking his thumb to help him out.

'I gets yer, chum,' he nodded. 'Yer wants to get married and settle down to a decent job, eh?'

'Yes . . . But I can't walk out on Gartell, he'd croak me. I know too much about what goes on at the Club. I believe he suspects me already of being a squealer.' He broke off and shivered. 'I — I'd 've gone to the police, only I've been afraid . . .'

'And this bloke Lang,' Mr. Walker said

slowly, 'where is 'e now?'

'At the club. Gartell's hiding him there I'm certain. And I wouldn't be surprised if his idea was to smuggle him aboard a ship he's got lying down the river.'

'Well, chum,' the junkman said at length, 'my advice ter you is ter come along o' me ter Scotland Yard.'

The other's face went white and drawn.

'Now, yer won't 'ave nothink ter worry about. I got a pal there, Inspector Wedge 'is name is. All yer got ter do is tell 'im wot yer told me. An' yer can take it from me, chum, 'e'll see yer comes ter no 'arm.'

'You really think so?'

'Sure as eggs. You and me'll go along together and you can put yer cards on the table. Come on, there ain't no time ter be lorst. Or that bloke Lang'll be 'oppin' it somewhere else!'

He bundled the still hesitant Hass out of the junk-shed and together they crossed the yard and went out into the street. As they did so a long-bonnetted black saloon car drew alongside them.

Mr. Walker was urging his companion

to hurry, when a chilling voice cut into his words.

'Hi, you two! Get into this car — quick! Unless you want trouble!'

Hass's face paled. 'Nick the Snake — ' he began, as the owner of that appellation got out and jabbed a blue-nosed automatic into his ribs.

'Get in! Both of you!'

Mr. Walker eyed the gun in his friend's ribs with disfavour and gave a quick glance up and down the street. But there was no one in sight who could come to their assistance. Defying a man with a loaded gun was rather like committing suicide, he decided.

'Seems this bloke's got the drop on us, chum,' he observed placidly, and moved towards the car.

Hass, trembling and white-faced followed.

The man who was driving Nick the Snake's car leant across and opened the rear nearside door. Then he turned back and kept his eyes on the road ahead.

Nick the Snake jerked the automatic hard against Hass's ribs again, a murderous glint in his ice-cold eyes.

Hass stumbled into the back of the black car after the junkman. The door slammed shut. The gunman jumped beside the driver and swinging round in his seat flourished the automatic menacingly as the car shot forward.

'Any tricks from either of you and you get yours!'

'Orlright, mate,' grinned Mr. Walker resignedly. 'Where we goin' . . . Bucking'am Palace?'

'Keep your trap shut,' snarled Nick the Snake. 'You'll soon know where we're taking you.'

His cold eyes never left his captives as the black saloon threaded swiftly in and out of the traffic. It attracted no attention and presently the driver swung into the direction of the luxuriously converted warehouse on the waterfront.

'Nice little place yer got 'ere,' offered Mr. Walker as they halted outside the Waterfront Club.

'Cut the cackle and go on in! Any tricks and this gun'll give you a bullet where it hurts!'

The gunman walked directly behind

the two prisoners as they entered the club. The doorman who admitted them scarcely gave them a glance. But a cold shiver ran down Hass's spine when that heavy door closed behind them. To his distorted imagination it sounded like a coffin lid being slammed into place.

Max Gartell was waiting for them when they reached his softly-lit — there were no windows to admit any daylight — and luxurious office. His fat, bloated face became purple with rage as his lieutenant related how he had shadowed Hass to the junkman's house. Gartell questioned Mr. Walker and after the latter had supplied him with the necessary information about himself he shot him a leering glance.

'Well, Mr. Walker,' he purred, 'I'll have a little problem for you, that'll take you all your time to solve . . . ' he smiled humorously, then turned savagely upon Hass. 'Same goes for you — you rat! You know what happens to squealers?'

'I haven't squealed. Honest I haven't,' gibbered the other piteously.

'Take 'em away, Nick,' snarled Gartell. 'You've got your orders.'

He pressed a podgy forefinger against a section of the decorative moulding of the wall. Noiselessly a panel slid away to show an iron staircase, which spiralled down into the depths of the old warehouse.

'One of the boys is waiting for you down below,' he added. 'He'll give you a hand with these birds.'

'Get moving, you two,' snapped Nick the Snake. 'Down the staircase, and remember my trigger finger's just itchin' for some exercise!'

Hass was the first to start the descent, and after him followed Mr. Walker. Not more than a step behind them came the gunman. There was a metallic click as the sliding panel in Gartell's office slid back into place behind the three men, and simultaneously the spiral staircase became ablaze with light, switched on from the office they had left.

In silence the prisoners descended. At the foot of the spiral stairway another of Gartell's lieutenants was waiting. He grinned at the sight of Hass's white. anxious face.

'Welcome home, George!' he mocked. 'I got a nice little room all ready for you!'

A short distance from the foot of the spiral stairway was a cellar-like room into which the prisoners were bustled. While Nick the Snake stood by, gun in hand, his companion bound and gagged them. To Mr. Walker's ears came the recurring sound of lapping water. He knew he was very near water-level, and his eyes dwelt upon a door at the far end of the cellar. Nick the Snake observed his gaze and laughed harshly.

'Later on tonight you and your squealer friend'll go through there. You'll both have a swift trip down river and then you'll be slung aboard a boat.'

He laughed again unpleasantly. 'You'll both look very pretty with a hundred-weight of lead tied to your feet when the skipper chucks you overboard! But you got plenty of time to think about it,' he added malevolently, ' 'cause that won't happen till you reach the open sea . . . '

And beckoning to his accomplice, whose work of tying-up and gagging the two captives was now completed, he went out. The other man followed slamming the door behind him. There came next the grating sound of a key being turned in the lock. Then the lights went out.

Mr. Walker and his companion were alone in the dark.

32

An artist in crime

Lee Burke, the portrait painter, sat before his easel in his sumptuous studio, which was situated in a quiet, residential part of Chelsea, close by the Embankment. That it was night made no difference to him. He was an eccentric and as such threw aside all the rules of his profession. Artists did not, generally speaking, paint at night. Daylight was necessary to their craft. But not so in his case. His spacious and lofty studio was fitted with daylight bulbs, which shed a weird glow over everything within range. Burke claimed he could paint as well by this light as the more conventional artist painted by natural daylight.

Although his real business was running a dope racket, the artist was undoubtedly a gifted painter of pictures. Numbered among his satisfied patrons were many of

Mayfair's most beautiful women. He liked his sitters to be young and pretty.

There was no ground for complaint on either count with the girl who posed now before his easel. In addition she was wealthy.

It flattered her vanity to think Lee Burke should beg her to sit for him. Still more flattering to her was the suggestion he conveyed that she possessed a definite attraction for him.

She had fallen for his lavish flattery but, incidentally, for him as well. In fact, one day soon, she hoped to be his wife. She did not suspect that he much preferred to remain single. A wife, in the peculiar circumstances that surrounded his nefarious trading, would have proved inconvenient. But it was part of his scheme to suggest that he was falling in love with her.

'My darling, you look exquisite,' he exclaimed, as he threw aside his brushes and palette and crossed to her.

'But let's call a halt for the moment and have a cigarette and a drink . . . Eh?' Then after a pause: You wouldn't like a pinch of 'snow', would you?' he added banteringly.

Mary Nash's pretty blue eyes opened wide. She had heard a lot about the dangers of cocaine, but had yet to meet anyone who possessed the illicit drug. Despite the warnings she had both received from her parents and read frequently enough in the Press there was to her something alluring about this innocent looking white powder which was able to excite the senses beyond belief. All of which the man with her was thoroughly aware.

'Does it really do all people say?' she asked innocently, accepting a cigarette from him, and blowing out a cloud of smoke.

He laughed and shrugged playfully.

'I'm not an expert, really,' he replied. 'But I'll be honest with you. I have taken cocaine — once!'

'Have you really?' Her eyes were alive with curiosity. 'What did it do to you?'

He laughed again. How easy she would be to manipulate when once she had swallowed the bait he dangled. Still, it

330

behoved him to play his fish carefully before he finally landed her. She must not slip from the hook.

'Its effect is beyond me to describe,' he replied. 'Except that I felt an ecstatic well-being with everything and everyone around me. I'm told, of course, to make a habit of taking 'snow', as they call it, is highly dangerous. Still,' he added with a laugh, 'it didn't do me any harm. But let me get you a drink.'

He mixed her a cocktail and raising his glass toasted her.

'To the prettiest girl in the world!' Solemnly he drained his glass.

'Oh, Lee, you're such a flatterer. I'm not all that pretty, really.'

'My dear, you're too modest. I am trying my best with this painting of you, but even so I fear it will not do you justice.' He sighed. 'Sometimes I wonder if perhaps a sniff or two of cocaine would buck up my inspiration. It has that effect, you know . . .'

Cunningly he was bringing the conversation back to where he wanted it. For quite a little while now he had looked upon this young girl, rich and spoilt as a very suitable 'client'. She was weak-willed, susceptible to flattery and suggestion. It should not be too difficult to start her on the drug habit. Once she had taken that step there would be no need for him to persuade her any longer. He knew she would come to him and beg for the stuff. They all did. And they paid for it, he saw to that.

She read nothing of the man's inner thoughts as she gazed frankly into his handsome face. She saw him only as the man she was becoming more and more infatuated with each time they met.

He sighed as he glanced at his watch.

'My sweet, we have another hour's work before us. Are you ready to go on?'

She smiled and nodded her willingness, finished her cocktail, crushed her carmine-tipped cigarette in an ashtray, and resumed her pose. Back at the easel the other painted mechanically, telling himself he would be repaid again and again, and very soon. A few more sittings, the same measured doses of suggestion regarding the delights of the forbidden drug and the girl would be in his power as surely as night falls upon the waning day.

But outside that lavishly appointed studio Fate was playing a hand. A hand in which the aces and trumps were hidden from Lee Burke's knowledge. A car had driven to the corner of the street. From it, muffled in a long coat and a soft hat crushed well down over his eyes, stepped Lang.

He muttered a word to the driver of the car who nodded and waited with engine running. Lang knew the whereabouts of Lee Burke's house. Gartell who had visited it on two or three occasions, had made him thoroughly acquainted with the geography of the studio and its surroundings. It would not be difficult to force an entry, do what he had to do, and make his escape all within the space of but a few minutes.

There was a diabolical purposefulness about him as he strode off into the darkness, his right hand gripped tightly about a gun. The weapon was fitted with a silencer. He knew he was about to make a last desperate throw for freedom. He had read in the morning papers of the arrest of Fenner and Elias Pringle, and the disclosure of Ashton's impersonation. He had also read of the latter's death a little while before.

And so it was imperative he should not fail Gartell, for if he did there was no one else left who could possibly help him. His teeth set, and his jaw drawn in a hard line, he moved stealthily forward.

No one observed him enter the gate of the house. No one saw him move off at a tangent from the pathway to the adjoining lawn. The studio, he knew, was at the back of the house. He was even aware that Lee Burke was, at that moment, painting the beautiful Mary Nash, for a fake telephone call that Gartell had arranged had drawn that information.

Lang did not worry about the girl. The business he was bent upon did not necessitate revealing himself. Not the way he figured it. He arrived outside the heavily curtained studio and pressed his face against the long french windows. He was not surprised to find them locked. Faintly to his ears came the murmur of voices, and an occasional laugh.

Quickly, he got to work. A tiny bead of light from a fountain-pen torch showed him the catch which secured the french windows. That was all he needed for his purpose. The thin thread of light was extinguished in a flash. A diamond cutter now appeared in his right hand, whilst in the other was a rubber suction cap that he pressed against a section of the glass near the catch.

It was the work of a few moments to cut away a small section of the window pane, just large enough to allow the passage of his hand. The suction pad held the piece of glass as the diamond cutter did its work and, in a moment or two, he was able noiselessly to place the fragment down beside him. A moment more and his right hand was fumbling with the catch holding the french windows shut. That, too, moved without the slightest noise to betray him.

Gently he pushed open the doors, just sufficiently wide to admit his body. He gripped the left hand curtain and drew it aside.

He caught a glimpse of the girl posed near the man he had come to kill, and he smiled. She was prattling away oblivious of the sudden death which stalked close behind her companion. Next into focus came Lee Burke. With his head half turned in Lang's direction he presented an admirable target.

Slowly the gun, fitted with the silencer, rose in the killer's right hand. His dark eyes squinted for a sight of that spot just behind the unsuspecting victim's right ear.

The trigger completed its movement. There was a flash, which brought a cry from the startled girl . . . a sinister 'plop' as the silencer muted the report and Lee Burke, without a cry, slithered to the floor.

The murderer turned to flee. But in his haste he forgot the window behind him was only partly open. He collided with it, stumbled and clutched wildly at the long curtains to save himself from falling. His weight brought them down. It all happened in a flash, but swift as it was the now terrified girl caught a glimpse of him.

He realised that fact with a snarl of rage. Well, it was just too bad for her. Nobody was going to know he was the killer of Lee Burke, he told himself.

Even as she opened her mouth to scream he blindly pulled the trigger again. The girl dropped down and lay dreadfully still. Breathing hard, his lips parted over his teeth in a demoniacal grin, Lang dashed out into the night.

A moment or two after he had disappeared, Mary Nash rose to her feet. Her pretty face was pale and she trembled violently, but she wasn't so much as scratched. In his panic-stricken haste Lang had missed her by something under an inch. And her sudden instinctive impulse to fall and feign death had saved her life.

She took one look at the man who lay inertly in front of his easel, and, stifling the scream that rose to her throat, she rushed to the telephone. In a moment she was dialling nine-double-nine.

33

The raid

The sergeant at Scotland Yard who answered Mary Nash's frantic call contrived to calm her enough to obtain a description of the man whose murderous bullet had slain Lee Burke.

'He shot Mr. Burke . . . then he fired at me,' she repeated hysterically.

'Right-o, miss. Please stay where you are until the police come.'

The police arrived within ten minutes. In charge was Inspector Wedge. He had chanced to be on duty when Mary Nash's urgent call came through, and had received the account of the killer's description from the sergeant who had taken it.

There was only one person who answered such a description he knew. That person was Lang. When Mary Nash herself told him what the man looked like by the powerful studio lights that had caught his face as he stood framed in the french windows, he was positive he had picked up Lang's trail again.

He listened patiently to the young woman's story, while the police surgeon knelt beside the body of the murdered man.

'He's dead all right,' grunted the doctor as he concluded his examination. 'Instantaneous,' he told Wedge, who had finished questioning the girl and went off into a detailed assembly of medical terms concerning the wound and the position of the bullet to which Inspector Wedge listened absently. It was the murderer who occupied his mind to the exclusion of all else. What had Lang to do with Lee Burke, he asked himself. Why had he killed him?

He took little interest in the work of the police photographers as they took picture after picture of the studio and the dead man. Neither was he interested in the fingerprint specialist's report that no prints were to be found on the latch of the french windows. Lang, he surmised, would have worn gloves. He turned to the girl again.

'Are you sure, Miss Nash, no words were spoken between Mr. Burke and the murderer? No threat — no recriminations?'

'He just appeared at the windows and fired at Mr. Burke who was standing before his easel. When he stumbled and dragged down the curtains I caught sight of his face, and he fired at me . . . '

The Inspector nodded. Why should Lang, already wanted for murder, callously shoot down a man whom, so far as the detective could see, was a complete stranger to him? Where was the connection? If only we knew that, the Scotland Yard man told himself, then he might know where to start to look for him.

Inspector Wedge was well aware Lee Burke had long been suspected of trafficking in drugs. Yet the man had worked so carefully that proof against him had never been forthcoming. Now, however, as the police began to search the Chelsea house, while looking for the motive for the murder, they found ample

340

evidence of the artist's nefarious activities in the handling of illicit drugs.

It was when his sergeant brought him Burke's diary that the detective picked up what he thought might be the clue he was seeking. As he turned the pages he suddenly came across an entry that referred to an 'offer' from Max Gartell 'to buy me out.' Against the entry was the record 'Turned him down'. On another page was: 'Max tried again. Suggested partnership'. And against that was written: 'Told him N.G . . . Must watch out for him. Dangerous customer.'

'H'm. I seem to be getting on to something,' murmured Inspector Wedge. 'Max Gartell . . . Gartell . . . Let me see,' he mused, 'we've had our eyes on that gentleman for quite a long time. He's interested in dope, too . . . but we've been waiting for a chance to pin something on him — '

He broke off with a low whistle.

Lang, as an inspector of police, had been at the Commercial Road police station and his duties there, automatically, would have brought him in contact with the Waterfront Club, of which Gartell was the proprietor. He would be known to him, for a certainty. It was a regulation duty for the police to make routine visits of inspection to all night-clubs.

Inspector Wedge closed the diary and sat down for a while. Fitting a fresh cigarette into his holder and lighting it, and closing his eyes, he began to theorize.

'Gartell is at loggerheads with Lee Burke,' he murmured to himself. 'Yes, that looks all right . . . Burke's entries in the diary suggest he anticipated trouble from that quarter . . . Even so, I still don't see where Lang enters into it? He comes here without any apparent motive, and kills Burke. What for? Why should he do that . . . ?' And then an idea struck him. 'Unless, shall we say, he was working for Gartell? Yes . . . *That* could fit in! . . . And if it does, what was to be Lang's reward for removing Gartell's rival? What could a man like Gartell give him in return for such a service?'

Inspector Wedge opened his eyes and rose suddenly to his feet.

'It's a long shot, but I'm going to take it,' he remarked thoughtfully to his sergeant, who nodded agreement, without any idea of what his superior officer was talking about. 'I've got a hunch I know where Lang is,' added the inspector, and he crossed to the telephone. He was quickly put through to Scotland Yard.

Briskly he gave instructions for the Waterfront Club to be raided. It was to take place that night and was to appear a normal raid, but the premises were to be surrounded, and no one was to be allowed to leave. He finished giving details as to how the raid was to be carried out, and then, replacing the receiver, turned to the sergeant who, wearing a puzzled look, had stood listening to him, and smiled a quiet little smile.

★   ★   ★

Gartell was in his most genial mood. Resplendent in his too slickly cut evening dress, with the ever-present purple carnation in his lapel and his fat podgy

343

hands aglitter with diamonds, he stood at the vestibule of his club, bestowing a smile here and a nod there to his customers. The smiles were for the benefit of those flashier members of the smart set who came to spend their money on indifferent champagne. The nods were for the special benefit of those unfortunate beings whose existence without dope had become unbearable to them. The nods reassured them that — providing they could pay — there would be ample supply of the forbidden 'snow' before the evening wore out.

In the restaurant beyond the softly-lit vestibule the bandleader was in gay mood, and his orchestra played the popular dance tunes with indefatigable zest. The shaded lights added a warm and colourful glow over the glittering silver and napery on the tables.

Business, despite the comparatively early hour — for a nightclub — it was only half-past ten — was distinctly good. Guests were arriving every moment, young and old, respectable and otherwise — most of the otherwise — they crowded in Gartell's establishment for an evening's enjoyment. Uniformed waiters padded swiftly and silently to the serving doors and back to the white-clothed tables. Champagne corks were popping. There was laughter and gay chatter on every side. Standing at the entrance to the restaurant to eye the crowd, Gartell rubbed his fat hands and grimaced with pleasure. Then he waddled back to his private office.

He found Lang waiting for him, a stiff whiskey-and soda in his hand. The look on his face told the nightclub proprietor he had carried out the errand upon which he had been sent.

'Well?' Gartell's query was a purr.

'I got him all right. Never uttered a sound,' grinned the other back at him. His eyes were blood-shot, and were like those of some marauding beast.

'Good. That should be worth a bottle of the best,' was the answer. And in a moment, the dope-trafficker was removing a magnum from its ice bucket and undoing the cork.

'Here's to a pleasant voyage. In a little

while you'll be well away from the shore of old England.'

'And a damned good job, too!'

They drained their glasses, and Gartell produced a box of his favourite cigars.

'Yes, I fixed him all right,' said Lang, lighting his Havana. 'He never knew what hit him or where it came from!' He grinned evilly. Then he added: 'Pity though I had to shoot the girl — '

The other quivered and his piggy eyes glittered in their folds of flesh.

'What girl?'

'Oh, she was posing for him. I wouldn't have done it, only she got a look at my dial.'

Gartell breathed more easily again and stuck his cigar between his thick lips. He shrugged his shoulders.

'That's your look-out, anyway. Pity you had to bungle the job like that. Still, if you stopped her talking, there's no harm done . . . Now listen. Your boat'll sail at midnight, on the tide. Leave everything to the captain — you can trust him all right. He's already got his orders from me.'

346

He dived a fat hand into the pocket of his coat.

'Here's your passport, all nicely faked. And here's the money I promised you.'

'Fine!' grinned Lang, pocketing the passport and the envelope containing crisp notes. 'Now, how and where do I get aboard your boat?'

'She's lying about a mile down the river. I've got a fast motor launch waiting below, hidden away. Just before midnight you nip into it . . . By the way, you'll find a couple of passengers going with you. They'll be quite harmless — tied up and gagged. You needn't ask any questions. They're going aboard with you — the captain's had his orders about them, too.'

He leered, and the other nodded understandingly. A couple of squealers the dopedealer was 'eliminating', he told himself. Suddenly he glanced up with an exclamation.

'What's wrong with that light . . . '

He indicated a coloured electric light bulb over the door of the office, It was flickering off and on repeatedly. Gartell looked up at it and casually shrugged his shoulders.

'It's a tip off from my men below. It means the police are raiding us . . . '

'The police!' The stem of the champagne glass snapped between the other's convulsively tightened fingers. 'Here?'

'Now don't panic,' purred his companion, with a greasy smile of self-confidence. 'We've been raided before. It's a common enough happening at nightclubs, you ought to know that! I've got nothing to fear — '

'But what about me?' The colour had ebbed from the fugitive's face. 'If they find me here . . . '

'Take it easy. Take it easy! They *won't* find you.'

And sitting down at his desk he hastily scribbled out a note. The other man took it with trembling fingers.

'It'll mean you'll have to get out of here a bit earlier than I'd arranged,' said Gartell. 'But it won't make any odds.'

The red light was twinkling more rapidly than ever now Lang could scarcely take his eyes off it.

'But if the police are here I can't leave at all!' He gasped hoarsely, gibbering with terror. The other man smiled at him contemptuously.

'There are other ways out than by the front door my friend . . . pull yourself together. In that note you've got I've ordered the skipper to sail the moment you get aboard. Now . . . ' He pressed the switch of the sliding panel. 'There's your staircase. You'll find someone below who'll give you a hand.'

Lang passed a handkerchief across his face to wipe away the perspiration that dripped down it. 'Is the motor boat ready?' he asked, and received a reassuring nod.

'It's moored to the hidden landing stage . . . ' the other held out a podgy hand. 'Good luck . . . I don't suppose we'll ever meet again. I hope you get through all right.'

They shook hands, and the other started his journey down the spiral staircase. The secret panel behind him slid shut, the lights blazed his path down the stairs, and there, at the bottom, as

Gartell had said, he saw one of the drug-trafficker's lieutenants waiting.

'The Boss has just 'phoned me,' the man said, as the other reached him. 'I've got the boat waiting. Give me a hand with these in here will you?'

He led the way to the cellar-like room where Mr. Walker and Hass lay.

Lang started as he saw by the light of the other man's torch that one of Gartell's victims was none other than the junkman. It was none of his business to ask any questions, however, and so he made no comment as he helped to dump the prisoners in the waiting motor launch. The other man started up the engine for him and pointed to the black mouth of the short tunnel that led to the river.

'Drive straight ahead,' he instructed. 'When you get into the river turn the wheel clockwise a point, that'll swing you to the right, then open up the throttle and keep going. The ship you want is the seventh one you'll see, lying downstream. The captain's keeping a look-out for you . . . So long.'

The fugitive lost no time in obeying the

instructions. Clambering in, he headed the motorboat straight at the darkness before him, which grew lighter as he approached it, until he was out into the river. A turn of the steering wheel and the boat swung obediently to the right. On either side of him a few lights blinked against the murky background of the warehouses lining the banks of the Thames.

In front of him he was able dimly to make out a number of red blobs strung out in the distance, telling him of vessels at their anchors, with their riding lights aglow. The seventh blob was his . . . It would not be long now, before the last and vital stage in his bid for freedom was reached.

He grinned exultantly and opened up the engines of the motorboat to full throttle.

34

Grand finale

When two police-vans filled with officers drew up without warning outside the entrance to the Waterfront Club, Inspector Wedge was not present. He had left the handling of the raid itself in the hands of another officer, while he with more important work in view, was in the rocking bows of a river police boat, trying to convince himself he was a good sailor. The river was choppy, for the tide was beginning to turn. But the detective was prepared to suffer manfully in the discharge of his duty.

Crouched behind him in the boat was a police-sergeant, and two river policemen. All were armed with automatics. Like a dark smudge the police boat waited in the shadow of a wharf, its occupants watching the old warehouse exterior nearby which housed the Waterfront

Club. There was no sign of a landing stage. It had rotted away long ago, but Inspector Wedge felt confident a man of Max Gartell's cunning would have some form of a getaway, in case of trouble. With the river flowing at his back door, as it were, what was more appropriate than that he should have a concealed exit there?

It was this conjecture that had prompted the Scotland Yard man to make use of the river police in this final casting of the net with which he hoped to ensnare the murderous fugitive.

Suddenly there came a shrill whistle from the region of the dark warehouse. It was the prearranged signal by which the officer in charge of the raiding squad told Wedge the police had arrived, and were going into action. He jerked out a command to one of the policemen in the boat.

'Shove that searchlight on! Quick! Keep it focused on the old warehouse.' Even as the officer obeyed and the dazzling beam spread across the choppy water and lit up the old warehouse the inspector's keen eyes caught a movement at the foot of the building, where it joined the water. The next moment the brilliant searchlight sprayed across a dark shape that seemed to have appeared from nowhere.

'There it is!' snapped Inspector Wedge. And he almost fell out of the narrow craft as the helmsman swung his control hard over and started her off in pursuit. The powerful throb of the other's engines came across the river to them.

'After it!'

Like a greyhound unleashed the river police boat leaped in pursuit. The ferreting eye of the searchlight dwelt on the fugitive. And that band of blinding light told Lang his escape had been discovered and he was being pursued.

With a snarl he dragged out his gun and aimed at the small white circle that was the beginning of the beam. He fired two shots and the searchlight was suddenly dark. Either his shooting had been deadly accurate or else the pursuers had switched off the beam for their own safety. With a grating laugh he turned to the controls again. His engines were more powerful than the other's, and he was steadily drawing away.

While in the police vessel, Wedge, convinced now by those shots that his hunch had proved correct and the fugitive ahead was in fact the wanted man ordered more speed.

'Faster! Faster!' he implored. 'And put that searchlight on again. He'll give us the slip in this darkness.'

'The engine's all out now, sir! And the searchlight's gone west! One of his shots smashed it!'

The detective's response was to pull a revolver from his pocket. Steadying his aim over the crook of his arm, he fired a number of shots at the speeding shape ahead of him. But the distance was too great. The powerful motorboat was drawing further out of range with every second. It looked as if, after all, Lang was going to give him the slip. There were ample opportunities of doing so in the darkness and the widening river.

Inspector Wedge went so far as to lose his admirable self-control for a moment and murmur a mild curse beneath his breath. All his theorising and resourcefulness which had led him back to the trail of Lang were to amount to nothing it seemed, for here he was helpless in a boat that was outpaced, and he could only watch the object of all his endeavours fade from sight. He was not to know, of course, there were two other passengers in the rapidly vanishing motorboat, and that his old friend Mr. Walker was one of them.

For hours the junkman had wrestled with his bonds flexing his arms with optimistic patience. Now it looked as if that patience might be rewarded, for, exerting himself afresh, at the same time keeping his eyes on the man at the wheel of the motorboat, Mr. Walker definitely felt something give. He drew a hopeful breath and wrenched again. Yes, there was no doubt about it, a knot was slipping. Inspired by this success, he wriggled determinedly. In another moment a loop of the cord around his wrists slipped over his ham-like hands. A few more wriggles and they were completely free.

His heart in his mouth, Hass, who had been unable to make any impression on his own bonds or gag, watched while his companion cautiously reached down and tackled the cords that bound his ankles. It did not take the junkman long to untie the knots and then release the gag that half-stifled him. His task completed, he lay still, wondering whether his actions had been observed by Lang — he had recognized him in the glare of the searchlight, and realized he was intent upon making a desperate getaway.

But the fugitive, his work cut out to steer the boat, had ceased to glance back any more, now he knew he was quickly widening the gap between himself and his pursuers. His gaze was concentrated on the river ahead and the ship he was making for and which was drawing rapidly nearer.

And so Mr. Walker's mighty crashing blow into the back of his ear caught him utterly by surprise. The blow, delivered with devastating force, well-nigh stunned him.

With a horrible groan he turned to face

this unexpected attack, his right hand reaching for his gun. Before he could do so another massive fist took him clean under the jaw. The blow had travelled from well below Mr. Walker's hip. It came up with all the power and poise of a man who knew how to make the most of a punch. All of the junkman's not inconsiderable weight was packed into that fearful wallop, and it connected with bone-crushing force. Its recipient crumpled at the knees, teetered round and then collapsed in a huddled heap.

Mr. Walker jumped to the wheel and swung it to the left.

'Keep smilin', Hass!' he bellowed throatily over his shoulder. 'We'll soon 'ave them bits of string orf yer, chum. Stick it, mate, while I sees 'ow I'm like as a bloomin' sailor . . . Lumme!' he added with a note of apprehension in his voice, 'I wish I knew a bit more about these 'ere yachts!'

He succeeded, however, in successfully turning the craft in a wide sweeping circle so it now began to race back towards the police boat.

'Ahoy! Ahoy, there!' he boomed.

And his voice came across the water to Inspector Wedge like a bolt from the blue.

'Walker!' he exclaimed in astonishment. 'How the — ?'

' 'S' orlright,' the voice came again reassuringly. 'I got Lang with me!' And then: 'But 'ow the blinkin' blazes d'you stop this 'ere boat?'

The officer beside the Scotland Yard man gave an exclamation: 'He doesn't know how to switch off the engine!'

'Try and tell him,' urged Wedge, and called out himself: 'Switch it off. Switch it off!'

'That's wot I'm tryin' ter do, mate — but I can't!'

The junkman struggled desperately in the dark to find a way to halt the careering motorboat's progress.

'I'll 'ave ter stop it me own way,' he muttered, and called back to Hass: 'Sit tight, chum . . . and wait for it!'

Deliberately Mr. Walker turned the bows towards the riverbank and charged at it. It was a drastic way of bringing his progress to a halt but it was highly effective. The boat came to rest with a shuddering crash as it hit a strip of muddy bank into which, more by luck than judgment, it had been guided, escaping the more formidable side of a wharf by a couple of feet.

' 'S'orlright!' bawled Mr. Walker cheerily as the police boat drew across. 'I've stopped the blinkin' thing! Lumme, but I don't 'arf bump inter some funny 'ow-d'yer-do's, though, don't I?'

* * *

'Any rags, bottles or bones . . . '

Mr. Walker uttered his familiar cry in his rich and fruity tones as he trundled his barrow round a corner into the busy Camberwell Road. His attention, however, was less upon his surroundings and the passing acquaintances with whom he exchanged greetings than was usual. It was the morning following upon his hazardous adventures which had ended in his hectic motorboat ride, and he was now busily engaged in reading all about it on the front page of the newspaper spread in front of him across his barrow.

His battered bowler hat tilted even further back on his head, he read the whole story of Lang's murderous exploits which had culminated in the cold-blooded shooting of Lee Burke. There followed an account of Inspector Wedge's brilliantly inspired raid on the Waterfront Club, together with Max Gartell's efforts to help the wanted criminal to escape. Efforts which would probably have been completely successful but for his, Mr. Walker's, intervention which had resulted in the murderer's capture.

All this he absorbed with the greatest interest, making sucking noises the while through his disreputable pipe, as if the story was being unfolded to him for the first time, and he had taken no active part in it.

'Yes,' he muttered slowly as he read of the exposure of Gartell's dope ring and the drug trafficker's arrest, 'Honesty's the best policy and no error . . . '

But his greatest satisfaction was derived from something not printed in the newspaper, which was the knowledge that the future of George Hass was assured. Now the menace of Gartell was removed the reformed ex-convict had every chance of settling down to marriage and a decent way of living.

It was with this gratifying thought uppermost in his mind that Mr. Walker carefully folded the newspaper, shoved it into the pocket of his capacious coat, and pushing his barrow, ambled off upon his daily round.

THE END

We do hope that you have enjoyed reading this large print book.

Did you know that all of our titles are available for purchase?

We publish a wide range of high quality large print books including:
Romances, Mysteries, Classics
General Fiction
Non Fiction and Westerns

Special interest titles available in large print are:
The Little Oxford Dictionary
Music Book, Song Book
Hymn Book, Service Book

Also available from us courtesy of Oxford University Press:
Young Readers' Dictionary
(large print edition)
Young Readers' Thesaurus
(large print edition)

For further information or a free brochure, please contact us at:
Ulverscroft Large Print Books Ltd.,
The Green, Bradgate Road, Anstey,
Leicester, LE7 7FU, England.
Tel: (00 44) **0116 236 4325**
Fax: (00 44) **0116 234 0205**

Other titles in the
Linford Mystery Library:

THE TOUCH OF HELL

Michael R. Linaker

The village of Shepthorne wasn't being gripped, but strangled by winter's blanket of snow and Arctic temperatures. The trouble began with a massive pile-up on frozen roads and a fireball of exploding petrol as a truck collided with a tanker in the garage forecourt. Then, from the sky, a huge military transport with its cargo of devastation crashed down towards the village. Hell was just beginning to touch Shepthorne . . .

SWEET SISTER DEATH

Frederick Nolan

The objective of PACT — a secret counter-terrorism organisation, is to eradicate the perpetrators of political assassination and terrorist acts, and Charles Garrett is their best weapon. A bizarre series of murders plunges Garrett into a deadly conspiracy mounted by the terrorist Leila Jarhoun — the leader of a suicide cell created to unleash a holocaust of death across Europe. Jarhoun always strikes where Garrett least expects, until finally she confronts him — three hundred and fifty feet above New York harbour . . .

THY ARM ALONE

John Russell Fearn

Betty Shapley was a local beauty, for whose charms three young men fell heavily. But her coquetry would lead to death for one of her admirers, Herbert Pollitt; a fugitive's life for another, Vincent Grey; and becoming a murder-case witness for the third, Tom Clayton. Inspector Morgan and Sergeant Claythorne investigate the death, and suspect Vincent Grey. So Betty, former pupil of Roseway College for Young Ladies, asks Miss Maria Black — 'Black Maria', the headmistress detective — to prove Grey's innocence.

MAN IN DUPLICATE

John Russell Fearn

Playboy millionaire Harvey Bradman is set an ultimatum by his fiancée: before she marries him, he must carry out some significant, courageous act. Amazingly, the next day the newspaper carries a full report of Harvey's heroic rescue of a woman from her stalled car on a level crossing, avoiding a rail crash! But Harvey had been asleep in bed at the time of the incident. And when his mysterious twin seeks him out, he becomes enmeshed in a sinister conspiracy . . .

KILL PETROSINO!

Frederick Nolan

It is the turn of the century. Lieutenant Joe Petrosino of the New York Police Department is a man with an obsession. Believing that there is a secret society controlling organised crime in America, he aims to expose the Mafia. With disbelieving superiors, he alone must face the feared Don Vito Cascio Ferro. Would-be informers are too scared to talk, but Petrosino gets his first lead with the discovery of a brutally murdered body in a New York alley . . .